The One

The One

EDWARD MILLER & J.B. MANAS

SOMERTON
PRESS

ACKNOWLEDGMENTS

We would like to extend our gratitude to our alpha reader team of advisors, including Dawn Mahan, Paula Berinstein, and Gary Cutler, whose feedback helped us craft a fun sci-fi thriller we hope our readers enjoy.

Thanks also to the immensely talented Kirk DouPonce of DogEared Design, for his reliably stellar cover art.

Thanks to Cassandra Denton (the "real" Cassandra Denton) for graciously allowing us to use her cool name in the book, and to Tom and Ann Beth Goldblum for their unending support.

And of course, last but not least, thanks to our wives, Heidi Miller and Sharon Manas, for putting up with us, and to the next generation: Stuart and Nicole Goldstein, Becki and Ben Gomez, and Elizabeth Manas. Thanks also to our ever-supportive family: Carl Miller, Mike Myers, Sophia Gomez, Gabriel Gomez, Alicia Gomez, Mason Goldstein, Nolan Goldstein, Maeve Goldstein, and Eric and Chris Manas.

EDWARD MILLER & J.B. MANAS

Praise for The One

"A sophisticated thriller that deftly explores the nature of belief, loss, and redemption within a highly entertaining package... an action-packed battle for the future of humanity."

- BestThrillers.com

"THE ONE was such a good story... with aliens and treason [and] also faith lost and found...The characters are well written and interesting... the pace is quick but not rushed... An excellent escape into a thrilling, unexpected read."

- Booksirens Reader

CHAPTER 1

BEGINNINGS AND ENDINGS

L uke Remington said his goodbyes and boarded his flight
back to Philadelphia. His four years as a chaplain in the
Navy had come to an end, and for the first time in his
life, he felt he could shout, "Hallelujah!" and actually believe
it. After all, it had been six long months since he'd seen his
family. He would remain a member of the Naval Reserve, but
for now he'd finally be getting back home to his wife and
daughter. That, and continuing the centuries-long family
tradition as a pastor at Saint George's Church. Ironically, he
didn't think of himself as particularly religious—admittedly an
odd thought for a pastor—but serving people was another
story. If he could help other people find meaning through his
efforts, then it was a venture worth sticking with.

As Luke strolled through the aisle toward his seat, other
passengers smiled or nodded to him, thanking him for his
military service. He smiled back, all the time thinking about
the hugs and kisses he'd get from Kathleen and Kayla upon
arriving in Philly. And, truth be told, he could really go for a
cheesesteak. He could almost smell it already. He made a

mental note to take the family by Joe's Steaks on his way home. He and Kathleen had been going there since they'd started dating. It wasn't lost on him that Kathleen had to practically be a single mom to Kayla in the time he'd been away, though his mother-in-law was no doubt lending a hand—at least when she wasn't driving Kathleen crazy.

As he passed through the middle of the plane, he glanced down to check his boarding pass and confirmed that he would be in seat 18A, a window seat. When he got to his row, he was happy to see that the seat next to him was still vacant. Hopefully, it would remain that way. He settled in and prepared for the eight-hour flight.

While he waited for the remaining passengers to take their seats, Luke reflected on the horrors he'd seen overseas. It would shake anyone up, even those who'd been career military men. Nobody should have to witness such tragedy and senseless loss of life. He thought about the futility of expecting the world to change any time soon, and that inevitably got him into questioning God once again.

Devoting his life to religion wasn't an easy decision for him. He was a born rebel, always asking questions and questioning the answers he'd received. Even as he got older, he questioned what he saw going on in the world around him: widespread famine, rampant injustice, man-made climate change, and continuous wars. Most of all, he questioned God. Why would a supreme being allow all the horrors in today's world to happen? To what end? It led him to the concern that maybe God wasn't as all-powerful as people thought. Either that, or the Lord of all things has a "hands-off" policy— natural consequences, as they say. He refused to believe all the bad things in the world were part of some grand plan.

Nonetheless, despite his skepticism, Luke decided he would follow his family's tradition and be a lead pastor at the same church his family had served in for the last hundred years. He hoped his teachings would make a difference, at least to a few people.

Luke was startled back to reality by the loud bang of the cargo doors shutting. The last few passengers were stowing their bags and taking their seats. The seat next to him was still unoccupied, and, with no further passengers boarding, it looked as though it might stay that way. Now *that* was a blessing! He'd actually be able to relax in peace and stretch out. Just as the doors to the airliner were about to close, the final passenger entered and a young man in a Marine uniform made his way back toward Luke's row. From a distance, Luke could see that the marine was tall and broad shouldered. If this man was going to sit in the seat next to him, say goodbye to comfort.

As the man passed row 15, Luke watched him glance up to confirm the location of his seat. That's when he saw the young marine's grotesquely scarred face. Such a shame. From Luke's much too frequent experiences ministering to patients in the medical units in Afghanistan, he recognized the scarring as coming from serious burns.

As the marine turned to sit in 18B, he stared at Luke for a moment. "Pastor Remington?" he said, as he took his seat.

Luke knew the voice was familiar, but when he looked more closely at the man's face, the disfigurement made recognition more difficult. He looked at the man again and then it dawned on him. He confirmed his suspicion by checking the name patch sewn onto the front of the uniform. "Sergeant Royster?"

"How crazy is this?" said the marine. "I can't believe I'm sitting here right next to you. I thought I'd never get a chance to thank you in person."

"You don't have to thank me," said Luke. "I did what anyone else would have done in that situation. You would've done the same for me."

"That's what I'm trained to do," said Royster. "But you're a pastor. That's not what you're trained for."

Luke remembered that day clearly, even though it was six months ago. He was in a Jeep that was second in line in a caravan traveling toward a base outside Kabul. Sergeant Royster was the passenger in the lead vehicle when it ran over an IED. As the mine exploded, the Jeep was instantly engulfed in flames. On pure instinct, Luke jumped out of his vehicle and was the first one to Royster. The Jeep's driver was clearly dead, but Royster was alive and screaming in pain. Luke grabbed him and pulled him out of the inferno to safety. Fortunately, while he did suffer some minor burns, Luke was otherwise unscathed by the incident. The truth is, if he'd thought about it, he probably wouldn't have risked it, but he was running on adrenaline. Luke had remained with Royster to comfort him while awaiting transport, and that was the last time he'd seen him—until now.

As Luke glanced down at Royster's hands, he noticed that they, too, had significant scarring. Poor guy probably had scarring all over his body.

"How are you doing, Sergeant?" he asked.

"Getting better every day," Royster said, smiling. "It's been a tough road. More surgeries than I care to count. Lots of rehab. But I'm finally going home, thanks to you. I'm thinking I'll do really well at zombie fests." Royster laughed. At least he had a sense of humor about it. With some soldiers, it's the only thing keeping them sane.

"Well, I expect a ten percent commission for all your bookings," said Luke.

Royster chuckled, then looked more serious. "Can I speak freely, Pastor?"

"Of course," said Luke.

"Truth be told, I was never really religious. But, when I woke up in the hospital and I was told that I was saved by a chaplain, I saw this as a real sign, a message from God that He's actually there and won't let me fall."

"Well, you know what they say. There are no atheists in foxholes."

"That's for sure. But maybe it was really Him telling me that if *I* can believe, then anyone can. Anyway, I'm going home to meet my newborn son for the first time. If it wasn't for you, whether it was God's doing or yours, my son would never have an opportunity to know his father. I'd never be able to hold his little hands in mine. I'd never—" Royster was getting choked up.

Luke was overwhelmed by Royster's comments and put a hand on the man's shoulder for comfort. "Pay it forward, my friend," he said. It occurred to Luke that Royster probably had a truer spiritual awakening than he'd ever had. Luke was still waiting for his. For now, he figured he'd change the subject.

"Where's home?" he said.

"For now, we're staying with my parents in Blue Bell, about an hour from Philly."

"Well once you get settled in and you get some time—"

Their conversation was interrupted by the captain of the plane announcing that the plane was next in line for takeoff.

"Well, look me up at Saint George's Church in Old City," said Luke.

"Oorah, Pastor," said Royster.

"Semper Fi, Sergeant."

Luke checked his seat belt, sat back in his seat, and, as the plane lifted off, he thought of seeing Kathleen and Kayla waiting for him in the arrivals lounge. The last time he saw Kathleen, she was considering cutting the long, blonde hair that made her blue eyes shine. He laughed to himself as he wondered whether he'd recognize her if her hair was cut short. Let that be the worst of his problems for the foreseeable future. He closed his eyes and drifted off to sleep.

◆

Luke was awakened by the captain's announcement that they had begun their descent into Philadelphia. He had slept through the entire flight. He looked to his right and saw that Sergeant Royster was still sleeping.

After what seemed like hours but was probably thirty minutes, the aircraft finally touched down. Royster stirred next to him, finally awake. Luke was practically dancing in his seat, anxious to see his wife and daughter. As the plane taxied and arrived at the gate, he gathered his belongings. As he prepared to exit his seat, he turned to Sergeant Royster and extended his hand.

"Take care Sergeant. And please stay in touch."

"It's Kevin," said Royster, shaking his hand vigorously. "Just call me Kevin. I'm telling you this was a real sign, our meeting here, Pastor. I'll look you up at the church."

"Sounds good, Kevin. I want to meet that family of yours."

"You will, Pastor. Like I said, a real sign."

As soon as the seat belt sign went off, Luke and Royster made their way out of their seats. "Now that," said Luke, "was the sign *I've* been waiting for."

Luke slowly followed Royster down the aisle of the plane, anxiously waiting as the passengers took their good old time ahead of them. Then, finally, they emerged out of the plane and followed the hallway to the arrivals area.

The moment Luke saw Kathleen's beaming smile, with her golden blonde hair and flushed face, he quickened his pace. Kayla was already running to him, her arms waving frantically as she screamed, "Daddy's home!"

He scooped up Kayla in one arm and put his other around his wife. He didn't want to ever let them go.

"Daddy, I hope it'll be a long time before you leave us

again," said Kayla.

"Are you kidding?" he said. "I won't ever be leaving you again."

Luke was astounded how Kayla had grown in the last six months and how she now spoke like a young adult, rather than like a toddler.

He looked to his left where the Roysters were celebrating. It wasn't until then that he realized he'd indeed had a hand in allowing their reunion to happen. Despite, or perhaps *because* of his role as a religious leader, it occurred to him that it's *people* who need to make a difference in this world. Everything we do in life impacts others, and we're all connected in ways we don't always understand. But we need to start with ourselves. He made a mental note to write a sermon about that.

After retrieving his baggage, Luke shook Royster's hand, and the two men introduced their families to one another. Then it was off to the exits toward the car. Luke was looking forward to spending the next few days doing absolutely nothing other than enjoying every moment he could with his family.

As they walked outside, Kayla tugged his arm. "Lucy!" she screamed. "We forgot Lucy!"

Luke turned to Kathleen. "Who the hell is Lucy? Did we get another kid while I was gone?"

"Lucy's her doll," said Kathleen, smiling. "It's only the tenth time she lost it this week."

"I just had her back there!" said Kayla, pointing back toward the baggage area.

Luke smirked at Kathleen. "You stay with Kayla and the luggage. I'll go look."

"But you don't know what she looks like!" said Kayla.

"My guess," said Luke, kneeling down to her level, "is that it's the only doll sitting on the floor by the luggage that looks totally bored."

Luke stood up and jogged into the baggage claim area and scanned the room. He walked all around belt C, where they'd picked up their luggage. It was then that he heard a male voice behind him.

"Rem-ing-ton," said the voice, pronouncing each syllable slowly and deliberately.

Luke turned to see a pale-skinned, middle-aged man sitting on the floor, with wild sunken eyes and even wilder brownish hair that looked like he combed it with an eggbeater. He wore a tattered grey suit and smelled like a trash bin. In his hands was an American Girl doll with blonde hair like Kayla's, which he stroked slowly.

"You don't remember me," said the man, still stroking the doll's hair, "but I remember you… Rev-er-end. You and your father." The man was grinning now, staring up at Luke. He was clearly either on drugs or was mentally ill.

"Who are you?" said Luke. "Is that my daughter's doll?" Luke approached the man and looked down at him. The man clenched the doll tighter.

"I'll take more than this doll," said the man, still smiling, as if he was keeping a big secret. "I'm gonna change your life."

"What are you talking ab—" Suddenly, Luke remembered who he was looking at. But he couldn't believe it.

"Nathaniel Dixon," said Luke. "You're Nathaniel Dixon." Luke remembered Dixon as a wealthy businessman who attended his father's church regularly. But Dixon was a normal guy. A bit pompous, but normal. What could have happened to him?

"I am," said Dixon, grinning like a maniac. "But now I'm someone else, too."

"I think you're hallucinating, Dixon. What drugs did you take?"

Dixon snarled as he leaned forward. "The drug of truth! It opened my eyes, Reverend. You should leave the church while

8

you still can."

Luke stared at him wondering what could have turned a normal guy into a lunatic.

"Okay, I'll keep that in mind," said Luke. "Now can I have my daughter's doll back?"

Dixon smiled and held up the doll. Luke grabbed it and began to walk away. Within a few seconds, he turned to say one last thing to Dixon, but the man was gone.

♦

Luke couldn't believe it was already Sunday. The week had flown by. He'd spent as much time as he could with his family and today was the day he'd be introduced as one of the new lead pastors at St. George's. Not that anyone would be surprised. Luke had spent every Sunday of his childhood there with his father, Charles, and grandfather, Richard, both pastors. And he'd served there for over a year as an assistant pastor before he'd taken the Navy chaplain role.

Sitting with his wife and daughter and watching his father at the pulpit, Luke's palms were sweating as if he were back in enemy territory in the Middle East. It had been a long time since he'd stood in front of the congregation, and now he'd have a much bigger role. His father was talking about him from the pulpit, telling silly stories of his childhood and leading up to his marriage and his time in the military. Funny, he remembered hearing a similar speech when he was a young boy. At that time, his grandfather was speaking about his father.

As his father called him to the pulpit, Luke rose and walked up the short set of wooden steps. He was amazed to see the church so full. It was so quiet, he could hear every little rustle of sound whenever someone shifted position, punctuated by the occasional cough. After shaking his father's hand, he looked at his mother, his wife, and his daughter and smiled at them.

Settling in, he turned his attention to the rest of the congregation.

"Thank you all for the warm welcome home," said Luke, instantly realizing that it was a silly statement, given that nobody could applaud in church. "It's a great feeling to be back among family and friends," he added. "As many of you know, I've been away for a while. But it's because of that time away, and the things I saw and did, that I hope to share some insights that I hope you'll find helpful. Or dare I say provocative. Because that's where real spiritual growth happens. To start with—"

His words were interrupted by a loud noise in the back of the church as the rear doors burst open. A man entered, and as Luke tried to make out who it was in the distance, people began raising their voices in the rear of the church. Then his focus cleared and his heart dropped. It was the lunatic from the airport, Nathaniel Dixon. Just what he needed on his first day as a lead pastor. Within seconds, a woman screamed, "My God, he has a bomb!"

Luke watched in slow motion as Dixon raised an automatic weapon in the air and began firing at nothing in particular. Pieces from the ceiling fell to the ground. People put their hands over their heads and many screamed in horror. Luke knew that sound all too well—the sound of chaos and terror. He'd heard it more than once in Afghanistan and it was a sound he'd hoped he'd never hear again.

Then the gunfire stopped.

"Now that I have everyone's attention," said Dixon, loud enough for everyone to hear, "I want complete and total quiet or I'll blow up myself and everyone with me. Everyone got that?" He looked around the room with wild eyes. He fired a few more rounds into the air for good measure and told everyone in the back of the church to get up slowly and move away toward the front of the church.

One man started running, and Dixon fired another shot in the air. Everyone screamed and huddled together.

"I said slowly!" shouted Dixon.

Luke's father had already begun walking toward the back of the church. Luke yelled, "Dad!" hoping to stop him, but it was to no avail.

"Nathaniel Dixon," said his father, "I know you don't want to do this. This isn't who you are. You have children that need their father. None of this is necessary. Let me help you, my friend."

"Your *friend*!?" said Dixon. "What have you or your church ever done for me? Your God has even given up on me. He doesn't care. He doesn't care about any of us. I'm afraid you haven't learned that yet, but today you will… *my friend*."

Luke watched as Dixon removed chains from a carry bag and threw them on the floor at Charles Remington's feet. Then the madman grabbed one of the women and put his weapon to her head, still looking at Luke's father. "Now be a good servant, Charlie and secure the doors to the church for me."

Luke had seen and heard enough. He made his way down the aisle towards Dixon. "Nathaniel!" yelled Luke. "Let me secure the doors. I'm the active pastor here today. It's my responsibility."

Dixon turned toward him and grinned the same evil grin he'd displayed at the airport. "I told you I'd change your life, Luke." His face turned more serious. "Now get on with it," he growled, "and lock the doors before I kill this poor soul and her blood will be the first to be on your hands."

Luke put his hands in the air. It was obvious that Dixon was psychotic, and the slightest thing could set him off and lead to disaster. He slowly knelt and picked up the chains and the locks from the floor and walked to the doors. "Okay, Nathaniel. I'll do what you ask if you do something for me."

"I already gave you your doll, Reverend. Don't push it."

"Let the women and children go," said Luke. "There are plenty of hostages here." Luke softened his voice and made eye contact with Dixon. He hoped there was still some sense of compassion left inside the man's troubled soul. "Whatever beef you have with me, or even with God, that's your right. But please let these other people go—at least the women and children."

Dixon stared at him intensely. Luke waited to see his response, but none came. He hoped he hadn't triggered some rage in Dixon and made things worse.

Luke didn't know what else to say and was mulling over his next course of action, when Dixon finally spoke.

"Okay," said the madman.

Luke couldn't believe his ears. "Okay? You'll agree to let them go?"

"Only the women and children," said Dixon. "With two exceptions. Your wife and daughter have to stay. After all, I need to make sure you have some incentive."

"Incentive for what?" said Luke.

"Don't look a gift horse in the gun barrel, Reverend," said Dixon, aiming the weapon at him. "You have to realize, life isn't about fairness, or good or evil, or even God. It's about power and who has it. And right now, that's me. So what'll it be, Reverend?"

"Alright," said Luke. "You win, Nathaniel." Luke turned to face the parishioners. "All the women and children come toward the exit. Women and children only." Then he addressed his wife, who he could see had a look of panic on her face. "Kathleen, please sit tight with Kayla, it'll be okay."

Luke jumped when Dixon fired another shot in the air. Everyone screamed and then quieted down as Dixon put a finger on his lips, hushing them. "If you value the lives of your husbands and fellow worshippers," said Dixon, "no tricks." Dixon made a show out of placing his right hand on what appeared to be a detonator. "Or all of you will really find God in your visit to the church today, you got it?"

Luke watched as some of the woman hugged their husbands. Kathleen and Luke's father insisted his mother leave with them. Many of them were crying as they made their way toward the exit. Luke hugged his mother as she left and told her everything would be okay. As the last of them left, he approached the doors and applied the chains to them. Then he turned to face Dixon. "Okay, Nathaniel," he said. "I've done my part, no tricks. Now what is it you want?"

"Follow me," said Dixon, as he began walking down the center aisle toward the front of the church.

Luke stood frozen, trying to think of a plan.

Dixon turned around and seemed surprised to see Luke still standing there half-dazed. "Did you not understand what I said? Get down here!"

With Kathleen and Kayla in the front of the church, Luke had no other choice, so he followed him. He glanced at the male congregants in their seats and could see they were shaking with fear. Some looked unsure of whether to do anything. He motioned for them to stay seated. He passed his father, who had his head down, praying.

Dixon paused at the front of the church, right near where Kathleen and Kayla were sitting. Luke watched as Dixon gazed at the large crucifix on the wall. Without turning around, Dixon said, "You know, Luke, you'd betray him just like Judas, wouldn't you?"

"I thought you weren't a believer," said Luke.

"Everyone is Judas," said Dixon, ignoring him. "So, you're in good company. There are no righteous people. It's all a big lie."

"Who's feeding you those ideas?"

Dixon turned toward him and scowled. Then his grimace slowly turned into a smirk as he shifted his gaze back to the cross.

"You'll find out soon enough," said Dixon.

Luke looked over at Kathleen, who was trembling as she held Kayla. Luke knew he needed to act now. He couldn't risk Dixon setting off the bomb anywhere near them. This was the ideal time with Dixon facing away from him.

Fortunately, Dixon wasn't wearing one of those hidden vests the pros use. This one was exposed and had visible wires. That would be Luke's best chance. Fortunately, he'd learned the basics of fieldcraft in his Navy training and he'd seen his share of bombs diffused. Only this time, he'd be the one doing the work. Taking a deep breath, he lunged forward and grabbed the wire that connected the explosives, ripping it away in one quick move. The force of his attack knocked Dixon to the floor, and Luke tumbled to the floor next to him—just as he heard the deafening sound of the AK-47 discharge, firing several rounds. Luke punched the back of Dixon's head, knocking him out, and that's when the horrifying screams coming from behind permeated his consciousness. Then silence. Only the sound of his father saying, "Oh God, no."

Luke's heart stopped as he turned, afraid to look. It was his worst nightmare. Kathleen and Kayla were both sprawled out motionless in their seats. He tried to get to them but could already see the blood and knew they were both gone. Out of the corner of his eye, he saw Dixon moving. Luke could feel his temperature rise as pure hatred flooded his senses. He clenched his fists and dove for the AK-47. With nothing but rage on his mind, he picked up the automatic weapon, stood up, and fired the entire clip into Dixon's face and body. Then in one last fit of fury he slammed the butt of the AK-47 into Dixon's skull. He dropped the weapon and knelt between his wife and daughter and collapsed onto the floor with the loves of his life. He felt his father's hand grip his shoulder, but nothing could comfort him now.

A noise startled everyone, a muffled explosion in the back of the church. Luke glanced up to see a SWAT team entering, their weapons drawn. As far as he was concerned, this was the end of the world. It was certainly the end of *his* world. He was numb, defeated, and full of hatred. Hatred at Dixon. Hatred at the church. Hatred at religion for creating lunatics like Dixon. And hatred at himself for not being able to protect his family.

He was so dazed he couldn't even think straight. He felt like he was at the beginning of a nightmare he couldn't escape from. Dixon was right about one thing. Life wasn't about fairness. It was about who had the power. A million thoughts were going through his head. But one thing he knew was that he didn't want to hear anything about God's elaborate plan or how important it was to have faith. If Afghanistan tested his faith, well this put a nail in it.

He thought about all the other acts of violence, in his city and all throughout the world. He didn't expect it to hit him personally.

He'd always felt there were four kinds of people in the world: healers, inspirers, followers, and fighters. He was too broken to heal anyone, and inspiring the pigheaded masses felt like a lost cause. He had too much rage to be a follower, so that left him only one choice. With any luck, maybe he'd end up back in Afghanistan, where he'd keep going until he got blown up. He just knew he couldn't stay here.

The way he saw it, if the human species was so committed to violence, well then, he'd dedicate himself to getting rid of as many evil bastards as he could. And there was only one way he knew how to do that. Something all the praying in the world couldn't accomplish.

As he watched the SWAT team approach, he stood up slowly and quietly, then stomped on what remained of Dixon's head one last time.

CHAPTER 2

A NEW PURPOSE

Luke felt numb as the SWAT team made room for the paramedics.

"It won't help," he said. "They're gone."

He could barely get the words out before he was consumed by a flood of emotions and memories. Shaking, he bent down to give Kathleen and Kayla a kiss as the paramedics covered their lifeless bodies and took them out.

"Pastor," said a voice from behind him. He turned to see a middle-aged cop in a white police shirt. "I'm sorry for your loss. Ain't nobody should ever have to go through something like this. I'm Lieutenant Brody."

"It's too soon, Lieutenant."

"You're right," said Brody, handing him a card. "I only wanted to give you this. I'd like you to come by the station in the next few days. Again, my condolences."

Luke examined the card while Brody walked away.

"Oh, one more thing," said Brody, turning around. "We had a lot of people who saw what you did today. I know it may not mean much now, but you saved a lot of lives today. A lot of people are gonna go on living because of you."

Luke nodded. "Thanks, Lieutenant."

While he understood the cop had a job to do, and he was appreciative of his sentiments, the truth was it was no consolation at all. He would've sacrificed every last one of those people if it would've saved Kathleen and Kayla.

Still in a daze, he proceeded up the aisle and walked out the door. Officers cleared a path for him to get to his car as a throng of reporters shouted out questions and condolences. Ignoring them, he continued to his car and left.

◆

The rest of the afternoon was mostly a blur. After returning to a house that was no longer a home without his family, he left and wandered around the city aimlessly. Finally, after stopping at a local luncheonette for a cup of coffee and pulling out the card Brody gave him, he decided to head to the police station. He may as well get it over with. Besides, the less time he spent in the empty house, the better.

As soon as he approached the door to leave the restaurant, he spotted a crowd of reporters outside. Someone must've spotted him going in. Hesitatingly, he opened the door, and immediately, he began getting peppered with questions.

He ignored them and turned to the right toward his car.

Up ahead, a young woman in an Air Force uniform was walking toward him with a little blonde-haired girl of about six or seven at her side. They reminded him of Kathleen and Kayla. As he passed them, the little girl stared at him and offered a slight smile. It was as if she could read his mind and was trying to comfort him. Still, he was too exhausted to smile back, though he attempted a weak one.

He turned around to see she was still gazing back at him, with a more concerned expression. He also noticed the reporters were catching up to him. He turned toward his car and ignored them until one question caught his attention.

"Pastor," said a female reporter, "why do you think God would allow such a tragedy to take place in a house of worship?"

He stopped in his tracks and turned around. He could feel the blood filling his veins as his fists tightened.

"Do you think God cares about this!?" he yelled. "I—"

He thought the better of continuing his rant as he turned to leave to the din of flash bulbs going off and a flood of audible gasps from the reporters.

As he walked to the driver side door of his car, he glanced back once more. The Air Force woman and the little girl had apparently stopped and were facing him now. The girl was still staring at him, but now she looked sad, almost heartbroken.

He felt a twinge of guilt as he got in his car and sped off toward the police station.

Within minutes, Luke was at the precinct. He walked in and could feel the eyes of the officers upon him. No doubt, everyone in the city was aware of who he was by now. He quietly acknowledged some of the officers as they came to him offering condolences. Brody must have seen him enter, as he came out from the back and motioned to Luke to follow him into his office.

As soon as Luke sat on the hard, wooden chair opposite Brody's desk, Brody handed him a document.

"I appreciate you coming by," said Brody. "This is my preliminary report that I'm forwarding to the DA. I'll keep this short and sweet, since I know you have more to worry about. After reviewing with witnesses, I've cleared you of any wrongdoing concerning the incident with Nathaniel Dixon. In fact, I'm recommending you for an honorary Sergeant Hendrix Medal of Valor. Usually that only goes to cops. I know you don't really give a damn about that right now, but you saved a whole lot of lives today and we all want to honor it. Not just for you, but as a way for the neighborhood to heal."

Luke didn't even know how to respond. In his entire life, he'd never been at a loss for words. Nor had he ever felt so broken and alone.

"Lieutenant, I appreciate that. I really do. But I hope you understand that I neither feel like a hero nor do I want to be seen as one. Whatever I did, whoever I may have saved, I failed to protect the two people I care about more than anything in this world. Nobody should be celebrating me."

Brody paused, apparently also at a loss for words. "I get that," he said. "Let's talk about it another day."

"Do you need a statement from me?" said Luke. "Because if we're done here, I have a funeral to plan."

"Just one thing," said Brody. "What was your contact with Nathaniel Dixon before this event?"

"I've seen him in the congregation, but nothing jumped out at me as strange about him, other than that he seemed a bit pompous."

Brody nodded. "That jives with what I've heard. I had to ask anyway. I talked to his wife, you know."

"His wife? What did she say?"

"He was an investment banker, a regular guy. Well, as regular as investment bankers can be. Pretty successful, too. But she hadn't seen him in a week and neither had any of his clients. She didn't report him missing because she'd been suspecting he was cheating on her for some time. So it seemed at worst, he was a scoundrel, but he didn't fit the profile of a shooter. Never owned guns, no history of violence. But then I did more digging and found out he lost his job a few weeks back and didn't tell anyone. Now, you tell me. Did he suddenly go nuts because he lost his job? Or was there something else behind it? Ordinarily, I'd say this was a crime of passion, and yet you haven't had any contact with him."

"You don't believe me?"

"That's the problem. I do believe you. And I know from eyewitness accounts, he wasn't there to target your wife and daughter. They were bystanders, more or less."

Luke tried to think back to the event, as painful as it was.

"I do remember something," he said.

Brody leaned forward with intense interest.

"When I arrived at the airport, he'd somehow picked up my daughter's doll. He gave it back, but he seemed deranged, not at all like I remembered him. In fact, I barely recognized him. He was sitting on the floor. I don't think I'll ever forget that crazy look in his eyes."

"Did he say anything?"

"He was rambling about how he was going to change my life, and he told me to leave the church while I still could."

"Why was he at the airport at the very time you landed?"

"Your guess is as good as mine."

Brody leaned back. "Well, it sounds like him being at the airport shows premeditation at the least. Either you were bizarrely unlucky enough to bump into him there and it triggered something in him, or he was specifically targeting your family because you were the closest thing to God he could get revenge on. I wouldn't rule out meth or fentanyl either. We haven't gotten the toxicology reports back yet."

"So what do we do now?"

"Not much we *can* do. The guy's dead, and it looks like he went nuts after falling on hard times and had it in for your family. 'Woe is me, God abandoned me,' and all that crap. But I can assure you we'll dig into what set Dixon off, and we'll get those toxicology reports. I'll let you know what I find."

"Thanks, Lieutenant. Is there anything else?"

"No," said Brody. "No statement needed. And if I do need something, I know where to find you. Once again, Pastor, I'm truly sorry for your loss."

"Luke. Just call me Luke."

"Luke it is." Brody seemed surprised by the request but stood to shake Luke's hand. Luke rose, shook the officer's hand, and left the office.

As he made his way out of the station, he was relieved to see there were no reporters this time around. Now he needed to head to his parents' house to talk to his father about arrangements. But first, he had another stop to make. After all, he'd made a decision—one that wasn't going to sit well with his family. And he couldn't waste another moment charting his new course.

♦

Satisfied with his brief, but important, stop, Luke pulled into the rear path behind his parents' row home to avoid being seen by anyone on the main street. He parked in their driveway on the left and entered through the basement door with his key. The whole situation was surreal, having come here so many times with Kathleen and Kayla. He still wasn't processing that it was real—that he'd never see them again.

Gathering himself, he walked up the basement steps and opened the door to the kitchen. As soon as he opened the door, his mother ran to him and embraced him. No words were said. No words *could* be said, as they sobbed into each other's shoulders.

His mother grabbed his face and looked at him with glazed eyes. "You did everything you could, Lucas. You saved dozens of people. Don't you dare blame yourself."

She grabbed his hand and led him into the living room, where his father was looking out the front window.

"Look at all of them out there," said his father, not realizing Luke was standing behind him. "Vultures, waiting for their prey."

"And here I thought I was leaving all the stress behind in

Afghanistan," said Luke.

His father turned around. "Luke, you've been all over the news," he said. "They've been hounding us constantly."

All of a sudden, his father broke down, the emotions of the day catching up to him. Luke put a hand on his shoulder to console him, as his mother went back into the kitchen to address a whistling tea kettle.

"They didn't deserve it," his father kept saying over and over. "They didn't deserve it."

Luke was emotionally spent.

"I'm gonna stop this from happening again," he said, clenching his fists. "In their honor."

His father looked up at him in confusion. "What are you saying? The man is dead."

"There are plenty of others like him, all around the world."

"Don't forget you're a man of the cloth, and all that goes with it."

"Well, it seems the cloth is no match for the sword."

"Well, here's a saying you may know. You live by the sword, you die by the sword."

"Then so be it. As long as I take some of them with me."

"Luke, you're talking nonsense. You're in pain, I understand that. Besides, the best way to honor Kathleen and Kayla—"

"—is to make sure it doesn't happen to anyone else."

"But you're a pastor. What did I say all those years ago when you were just getting started? Your number one duty—number one—is to bring peace."

"And that's exactly what I'm doing, in the most direct way possible. I'm doing something about it, Dad, I'm not just talking about it anymore. I'm leaving the church."

He could've predicted his father's reaction, which was an expression of shock.

"Leaving?" said his father. "Do you think this is what

Kathleen would've wanted?"

"What about all the other Kathleens out there? The ones who won't have a choice when some madman comes their way, whether it's a terrorist or someone with a screw loose? The whole world has gone crazy, Dad."

"You can't drive out darkness with darkness, Luke. Doctor King said that. You need light to do that."

"Doctor King was killed by a madman too."

His father sighed.

"Listen to me, Luke. You're distraught. You're not thinking clearly. This isn't the time to make a decision of this magnitude."

Luke tried to remain calm, but it wasn't easy.

"Dad, this is the perfect time. I've never been so clear about anything in my life. How can I rightfully stand in front of a congregation— especially in *that* church—and preach about a god that obviously isn't listening?"

"We can get a new building, just—"

"It's not about the building! I can't do this anymore. I'm done."

His father looked down, seemingly defeated, but then glanced up at him again.

"Luke, this is a tough time for all of us, and especially you. You're my son. I'll support you in whatever decision you make. Just don't shut us out. We're here for you, I hope you know that."

"I do, Dad. Thank you."

"May I ask what you intend to do, exactly?"

Luke nodded.

"I've decided to return to active duty. I've applied for training to become a SEAL."

"A SEAL!?" said a bellowing voice, coming from the top of the steps.

He turned to see his grandfather coming down the stairs

from the bedroom.

"Your grandfather's been staying with us," said his father.

"Lucas, have you lost your mind?" said his grandfather, stepping into the living room. "The good Lord has reasons for everything, even the horrible thing that happened today."

Luke threw up his arms.

"Do you have any idea of the training that requires?" said his grandfather. "You don't even know if you'd get approved."

"I'm already approved," said Luke.

His father and grandfather looked at him as if he had two heads.

"I met with your friend, Admiral Wilcox, just before I got here," said Luke. "They're giving me credit for my chaplain service. I just need about three more years of training and I'm in. Assuming I pass, which I will."

"Less than thirty-five percent do," said his grandfather.

"The others don't have my motivation, do they?"

The admiral had been a family friend for decades, as both families were from the area and had been serving in the Navy in various capacities for generations.

"Lucas, you need to think about this," said his grandfather. "I'll talk to him and explain that y—"

"I already have my orders," said Luke. "I ship out the end of this week."

◆

The days leading up to the funeral were a blur, but the funeral had been even tougher than Luke had expected. The hardest part was the viewing, not only seeing his wife and daughter for the final time, but also having to set foot in the very church where everything had happened. The constant media attention every time he'd stepped outside didn't help either, though Brody had graciously arranged for police limits to keep them at bay. He was surprised to have run into Kevin Royster and his family at the service. He hadn't seen them since the airport and made a mental note to follow up with Royster as promised.

Now that he was back at his house, he tried to focus on preparing for his trip. It was difficult, with reminders of Kathleen and Kayla everywhere in the house. He couldn't even walk in Kayla's room, and kept the door shut. And he'd slept on the sofa at night. Still, he couldn't help but feel like they were with him, which gave him some level of comfort, but then he'd get hit by a tidal wave of grief.

He knew the next three years would be the most trying and grueling of his life. But it would also focus him and give him purpose. There was nothing left for him here. Fortunately, he'd always kept himself in shape and worked out every day, but he had no illusions as to how difficult this would be, both mentally and physically.

He thought of all the injustice and violence in the world today—the atrocities and corruption in third-world countries, the unrest in the Middle East, threats from the East, the rise of authoritarianism, the hovering specter of fanaticism, and the mass shootings in schools, malls, and now his own church. For sure, there were plenty of violent lunatics to deal with. But dealing with violent lunatics was his purpose now, and nothing or nobody was going to stop him.

CHAPTER 3

ARRIVAL

Three Years Later

The past thirty-three months were even more difficult and grueling than Luke had expected, but now, as he sat waiting outside the deputy commander's office at the Naval Special Warfare Training Center in Coronado, he was looking forward to the next steps. As he thought about it, two hundred recruits had started in his class, but only sixty had finished. He knew just how fortunate he was to be one of them—though it wasn't just fortune that got him through training. He'd worked for it like nobody else through the most physically and mentally demanding exercises he'd ever experienced. Now came the payoff. Today, he'd find out his rank and assignment.

Because he'd completed a three-month sniper program that he'd been selected for after his initial training, he was expecting to be placed in the heat of action. After all, his long-range target shooting scores were impeccable, at least from what he was told. Of course, once he was assigned to a team, he'd then get a thirty-day leave, so it would be a bit of time before he got started. Still, as emotional as it would be, he was looking forward to going back home to Philly to see his parents and grandfather, and perhaps catch up with some old friends. It had been quite a while since he'd seen any of them.

The door to the deputy commander's office opened, and the executive assistant, Lieutenant Gallagher, a short, red-headed woman, signaled for Luke to enter.

"Admiral Hargrove will see you now," she said, smiling.

"Thank you, Lieutenant," he said, heading into the office and shutting the door behind him.

Standing at attention in front of the deputy commander, who was seated at his desk, he saluted. "Lieutenant Remington, reporting as ordered, sir."

Hargrove saluted back. "At ease, Lieutenant," he said. He had a slight Southern accent and was as stone-faced a man Luke had seen, even in the military.

Luke put his hands behind his back and stood at ease, watching intently as Hargrove flipped through his file.

Hargrove glanced up. "I have to tell you, Remington. I didn't think you had a chance in hell of getting through your training. A former chaplain? When Admiral Wilcox told me you wanted to be a SEAL, I thought it was some kind of joke. I don't mind telling you I disagreed with his recommendation. I thought it was a knee jerk reaction to what happened to your family. To be perfectly honest, I still do. I'm deeply sorry about what happened, by the way."

"Thank you, sir." Luke wasn't sure how else to respond.

Hargrove gazed at him as if judging his worth as a SEAL. "As a chaplain, you risked your life to save an injured marine in Afghanistan. That's impressive, but a single incident doesn't qualify you to be a member of one of our country's most elite forces."

"I understand that, sir."

"Let me finish, Remington. You had some of the highest scores in your class, across the board. In marksmanship, you qualified for the sniper program, which I must say shocked the hell out of me. Of course, qualifying and passing it are two different things. I see you completed it. Did you receive your scores yet?"

"No, sir, I haven't."

"Well, I have. Your scores are higher than any I've seen in years. I've got to hand it to you, Remington. You proved me wrong. Whatever your reason for joining, I'm damn glad you did. I'm assigning you to DEVGRU."

"DEVGRU!?"

"That's right," said Hargrove. "You'll be stationed in Virginia Beach."

Luke couldn't hide a slight smile. DEVGRU, which stood for Development Group, was the Navy's component of JSOC, the Joint Special Operations Command, which referred to the team as Task Force Blue. The team was legendary for having the most elite marksmen in the world. Their operations were classified, but they focused on counterterrorism, overwatch, intelligence, and taking out specific, high-profile targets. SEALs often still called the team SEAL Team Six, even though SEAL Team Six was officially dissolved in 1987 when DEVGRU was created in its place. DEVGRU often did off-the-grid, or "black" operations, directly under JSOC—in essence, the president's secret army used for highly classified and sensitive or pre-emptive operations. In other words, the usual rules often didn't apply.

"That being said," added Hargrove, "you won't retain your rank of Lieutenant and will be given the rank of E-6 Petty Officer. Captain Martinez is your team leader. You'll meet him once you get to camp. They'll be glad to have you. Like I said, best damn marksmanship scores I've seen in a long time, and I've been at this since before you were in diapers. Well done, Petty Officer Remington."

Luke was stunned. His emotions ran the full gamut. On

one hand, he wanted to jump up and down like he won the World Series, but then he'd remember why he was there in the first place. Either way, he had to contain himself. He remained stoic and saluted crisply. "Sir. Thank you for your trust in me. I will not let you or our great country down."

Admiral Hargrove returned the salute. "Now get out of here. You've got a well-deserved thirty-day leave coming to you. Dismissed."

Luke exited the deputy commander's office and headed back to his barracks. He had a lot of packing to do to get ready for his flight home, and couldn't wait to let his family know he had the highest marksman score of all the recruits. After all the trials and rough patches he'd been through in his life, Luke finally felt something he hadn't felt in a long time. A sense of purpose.

◆

Luke grabbed his bags and headed out to the main gate. A jeep was waiting to take him to the runway to catch a C-130 Hercules. He would be landing at Lakehurst Maxfield Field, about a half hour from Trenton, New Jersey, where his father would pick him up. Then he could relax and spend a month with his family. He hopped in the passenger side of the jeep and chatted with the driver about his plans during the leave as they made the ten-minute drive to the runway. The huge C-130 was already on the runway and waiting for him.

Luke exited the jeep and headed toward the huge transport. Just as he was about to climb the stairs to board, one of the pilots approached him.

"Petty Officer Remington," said the pilot. "I've been informed by Admiral Hargrove to notify you that we have a level-one threat and all leaves have been canceled. You're to report to HQ immediately for a briefing and immediate deployment."

Luke stood dumbfounded. He was annoyed with the change of plans. But, for his leave to be cancelled, it could only mean one thing. There was a serious problem somewhere and that's what he signed up for. He headed back to the jeep, which fortunately hadn't left yet.

"Back already?" said the driver.

"Don't ask," said Luke.

As they rode back to Admiral Hargrove's office, Luke's mind wandered as to what the level-one threat could be and where he'd be headed.

As soon as he exited the jeep, he could see other officers entering the command center along with several members of the SEAL teams. They were led to the briefing room where they took a seat and waited for the CO. They all sat in silence, waiting. Luke wondered why it was such a small group. There were maybe thirty people at most.

The door opened and the CO entered the room. All the officers snapped to attention and waited for Hargrove to speak.

"At ease," said the deputy commander. Luke watched intently as Hargrove began speaking.

"This briefing is for DEVGRU and select senior staff only. What I am about to say is classified Top Secret. Today at zero-eight-hundred hours local, we received a report from Joint Special Operations Command that there is credible evidence that a terrorist attack in the form of activated Russian sleeper agents has been planned at the United Nations next week during the Global Summit. This summit, among other things, features topics such as nuclear disarmament, cyber-defense, and satellite defense."

Luke couldn't believe what he was hearing. Russian sleeper agents in today's day and age? What would they do, wander in with bombs and machine guns?

"These agents will not look or sound like Russian soldiers or dignitaries," continued Hargrove, reading his mind. "More likely, they'll look and sound like everyday Americans. Schoolteachers, factory workers, seemingly innocent bystanders. Hell, there may be little old ladies. For all intents and purposes, this will look like a domestic terrorist event. There could be hidden explosives or even inside support. By treaty, this is international territory on American soil, so you can imagine this is a highly sensitive operation. All those in this room will be assigned duties in the theater of operations and will be given Top Secret clearance. We'll be providing overwatch, intelligence, and possible intervention. Once you arrive, you'll meet with members of the CIA and JSOC, where you'll be briefed further and given your codes. We move out in four hours. Dismissed."

As Hargrove turned and departed the stage without addressing questions, Luke left the meeting in stunned silence. Still, he was honored to be able to make such a difference so soon. Likewise, the others around him seemed more proud than concerned. He didn't think the SEALS operated domestically, but then again, the UN was a unique situation and DEVGRU specialized in off-the-grid operations. In any case, if he could help protect the country from harm, he was all for it.

◆

Today was the day of the planned meeting at the United Nations. Luke's team had been assigned to overwatch duty on the rooftop of the low-rise UN General Assembly building where the summit was being held. From here he could see the large circular fountain and flag-lined lawn where a crowd was already assembling. To his left was the 39-story centerpiece of the UN Headquarters known as the Secretariat Building.

Multiple news helicopters hovered above, some of which he knew to be secretly manned by military personnel, including Delta Force snipers.

Luke had been briefed from command that a team of CIA operatives posing as foreign dignitaries would arrive first. Considering the threat was deemed credible, it was arranged that the real dignitaries would arrive an hour later once it was deemed that the decoys were safe.

Using his Navy-issued Steiner M2080 binoculars, Luke surveyed the area below. Through his headset he could hear communication from his team, plus they had men on the ground with high-powered microphones that could pick up conversations in the crowd. Listening devices were set up inside the building as well. There was a line of news vans parked along the street, he assumed all pre-authorized. Scanning the crowd, he spotted a group of four men running on the far side of the fountain. He put down the binoculars and picked up his high-powered spotting scope to get a better look.

It was just some teens horsing around.

Just then, Captain Martinez's voice came through his headset.

"The package is en route. Repeat, the package is en route."

That was code-speak that the caravan of CIA decoys was about to enter the area in about ten minutes.

Luke switched over to his binoculars and scanned the crowd again. He was particularly looking for patterns. For instance, groups of people, together or separate, wearing similar clothes or hats or some other item to mutually identify in a coordinated attack. Lone actors who appeared to be talking on Bluetooth or texting or who seemed particularly preoccupied or nervous. People carrying items that looked like a possible container to store weapons. Aside from that, Captain Martinez had said to just keep an eye out for anything unusual or suspicious. It was like playing *Where's Waldo?* without the benefit of knowing what Waldo looked like. The obvious suspects would be anyone trying to get past the security barriers, but those were well-guarded.

"The package is arriving," said Martinez's voice over the headset.

Luke gazed out through the binoculars and saw the convoy of black limos approaching in the distance. The news helicopters hovering overhead rattled his headset—though the sound coming through the earpieces was fed by the mics focused on the ground. He tried to stay focused amidst the jumble of sounds and activity.

As the limos approached, his heart quickened as he scanned the crowd below. His breathing grew more frantic with every second, knowing that something could happen at any time. He kept scanning.

Scanning.

Scanning.

So far, nothing.

Then it came without warning. A massive explosion in the air rocked his whole body, knocking him backward. He shook the cobwebs off and looked up to see a huge fireball in the sky and a helicopter falling to the ground below. Everyone was panicking and running in all directions. What caused the explosion? In an instant, he got his answer. Some kind of rocket fired from one of the news helicopters flashed across the sky, taking out another copter. Then a rocket from another copter took out yet another target.

Luke glanced down at the open field and street and spotted a bunch of men in black uniforms and masks rushing out of the parked news vans and heading toward the limos. They sure weren't newsmen, and they were brandishing heavy-duty assault rifles. It seemed the copter attack was just a diversion. He picked up his rifle and got them in his sights. He had a clear shot of three of the men and took them out in rapid order. But several others vanished into the mob of people. He couldn't risk hitting civilians. He'd wait until they cleared the crowd. Then he'd get them.

From all the intelligence reports he'd been given, he felt it was unlikely these were Russian sleeper agents. He wasn't sure who they were, but this wasn't how the Russians operated. They were far more subtle than that.

Finally, he spotted the other men. His eyes followed them as they made their way to the edge of the crowd. He had his finger poised on the trigger. He had the lead man in his crosshairs. At once, a blinding light appeared, completely wiping out his vision. His first thought was some kind of nuclear attack. A deafening low hum penetrated his ears. He lifted the headset and still heard it. Then, there was silence. An eerie silence, like the calm before the storm.

The blazing light began to dissipate. He gazed through the high-powered scope on his weapon and was almost afraid to look. As his vision returned, he thought he might be hallucinating. He had to close his eyes and open them again to be sure. Because, amid the massive crowd below who appeared to be mostly in shock, a lone figure stood in a white robe and long, flowing dark hair. If he didn't know better, he'd say it was Jesus. But once the figure spoke, there could be no doubt. Whoever or whatever it was, it was no ordinary man.

"Be still, my brethren," said the strange visitor, his voice calm yet bellowing at the same time. The sound of his words echoed throughout the area. Luke could hear every syllable without his headset. Still, he put the headset back on, so he wouldn't miss anything. Little by little, the crowd quieted down and stopped running. It was clear they were as confused as he was. Nobody was quite sure what they were witnessing.

The mysterious figure turned and slowly walked toward a few of the black-clad terrorists who still had their masks on.

Were they with him? Luke got his answer when they lifted their weapons and aimed them at the strange visitor. At first, they just stared at him, frozen. Then the robed deliverer turned his head toward two other terrorists who were off to the side. They, too, aimed their weapons. Luke observed quietly and held up his arm to prevent any nearby men from his unit from firing quite yet. The supposed deity raised his arms toward the skies while he kept his gaze on the two groups of armed men.

"Give yourselves to your Father in Heaven," he said, "for He already knows your sins. Seek forgiveness among your brethren in the presence of the Lord."

One of the men broke the silence by firing his weapon at the self-proclaimed Jesus, as people screamed. Then another terrorist from the other group did the same. It seemed to have no effect. Almost immediately, two snipers from Luke's team shot down the two terrorists who'd fired. More people started panicking, but then the robed stranger, apparently unharmed, raised his arms, quieting the crowd once again.

"Hold your fire," said Martinez to Luke and his team through the headset. The booming voice spoke out once again.

"Let the keeper of the depths of the Earth consume those who have sinned today in the presence of the Lord; for those who cast away the Lord have spoken their allegiance."

Before Luke could even think about what that meant, a magnificent light emanated from the arms of the great speaker, and simultaneously from the ground below. Luke's heart began to pound, as, for the first time, the reality of what was happening set in. Was this a Biblical moment he was witnessing? The light traveled through the crowd like a glowing snake, selectively encircling the armed men as if it were the hand of God Himself. Or perhaps something more sinister.

Another of the men fired at the robed figure in

desperation, though the bullets clearly had no effect. Bloodcurdling screams emanated from the terrorists' mouths as their bodies turn to ash and disintegrated into thin air. Nothing remained of them as the encircling light vanquished, leaving only their weapons on the ground. Then the weapons disintegrated as well. The hordes of people watching in awe stood in stunned silence.

"The time that has been foretold is upon us," said the echoing voice, "as I bring joyful ascension to some and the eternal rest of darkness upon others." Luke redirected his binoculars toward the man, who certainly seemed to be the true Jesus, erasing any doubts he'd had in his mind. As far as he was concerned, the deity was three years too late.

The silence on the grounds of the United Nations was chilling. Smoke rose in the distance from the downed helicopters. The other copters were nowhere to be seen.

"Whosoever shall walk with me," the supposed savior continued, "and drink of my waters, shall not perish, and shall have everlasting life in the great cosmos. This I have promised, as my Father has promised, for I and my Father are one." The apparent messiah gazed around at his newfound followers. "None are excluded," he added, "and all who follow your shepherd shall be forgiven your transgressions."

Luke watched as the man held out his arms, and the assembled masses of all ethnic backgrounds begin to fall to their knees and bow. All but one little flaxen-haired girl who came forward slowly. She appeared to be about eight or nine.

Luke picked up his binoculars to get a better look. Something about the girl looked familiar. Then it hit him when he saw her mother trying to break through a row of police to stop her. It was the same little girl who had looked back at him with sadness after the tragedy of three years ago. What on earth was she doing here?

He watched as she approached the robed deity.

"You're not him," said the girl. Luke could hear her quite clearly through the headset.

The figure gazed down at her calmly.

"Young one," he responded, "have you not seen the miracles before you? Do you not trust your own eyes?"

"I don't trust *you*," she said. "You're not who you say you are. You claim to be of God, but you're not."

The Jesus figure smiled and looked around at the crowd. "From the mouth of a child," he said to those present. "Forgive her."

"He'll come for you, you know," she said.

"Who comes for the son of man?" said the robed one, whose expression remained stoic as his eyes began to glow.

"The one," she said. "The true one." She stood defiant. "I've seen it."

The figure raised his arms once again and looked around at the hordes of people, ignoring the young girl.

"Let all who stand before me, including deniers," he said, glancing briefly at the child, "know that I will bring peace to those who follow. Come with me. Be among the first to rejoice in the house of the Lord. Or suffer of your own volition."

The miraculous visitor turned and began walking away as the girl stood and stared. About a quarter of the bystanders began to follow him as he moved slowly and calmly toward the street, his flowing robe giving the appearance he was gliding. Even the police stood dumbfounded, and a couple of them joined the crowd of followers. The military personnel stood down, and a few of them even followed. Nobody dared to defy such power. As the herd marched with their new shepherd across the street and away from the scene, Luke's mouth dropped. He couldn't believe his eyes. They seemed to fade into thin air. All of them.

The remaining crowd let out audible gasps as they watched, horrified. A few ran to catch up with the departed, apparently making last-minute decisions, but they were too late. Luke couldn't help but wonder. Did they get lucky? Or did fortune favor the ones who took the leap? Though a small part of him wondered if this was for real, something told him there was more to this supposed messiah than meets the eye, especially after what the girl had said. And how odd it was that he should cross her path twice in his life. Could it have been a coincidence?

Just then, he was distracted when he noticed three men in black suits grab the little girl and pull her back behind the barricades, toward where her mother was standing. He watched as they dragged her toward the building and ordered her mother to join them. Luke froze as the young girl abruptly turned her head and appeared to stare directly up at him. The hairs on his neck tingled as her eyes locked with his, even from a hundred yards away. Through the binoculars, he could see she was about to say something to him. And in the headset, he could hear her words clearly and precisely as she spoke.

"Luke," she said, "come find me."

CHAPTER 4

AFTERMATH

Per Captain Martinez's orders, Luke had headed to ground level to join the rest of his unit and await further instructions. Meanwhile, he observed as police tried to restore order to the confused citizens while at the same time keeping reporters at bay. It was mass chaos. Finally, Martinez approached.

"Seems they have the situation about as under control as it could be," said Martinez. "Which is to say, barely. JSOC is classifying this as an *unidentified terrestrial phenomenon*."

"Well, that's a new one. I would've loved to have been in the meeting where they made that one up."

"Yeah, me, too. For now," continued Martinez, "we'll make sure those news vans are clear. Then we'll investigate the area where the crowd disappeared. JSOC orders are clear on this. This is strictly an area check for human hostile parties. We're to leave the study of the phenomenon itself to the Army scientists."

Luke spotted the young girl and her mother off to the left. They were being questioned by the men in dark suits as two policemen stood guard.

"That's the girl who spoke out," said Luke.

"And it's being addressed by the proper authorities," said Martinez.

"Captain, I know her. I've met her before. I believe she has pertinent information. Permission to approach her, sir. She'll talk to me."

Martinez hesitated and shook his head. He looked like he was about to reject Luke's plea. Then, to Luke's surprise, he said, "Permission granted."

Luke immediately headed to where the men were questioning the girl. As he approached, she turned her head toward him and smiled. Her sparkling blue eyes were like sapphires. One of the men jumped in front of her and came forward, holding his hand up to stop Luke.

"This area is off limits," he said. He had a grotesque scar that ran from his left eye down his cheek.

"I'm here to question the girl," said Luke.

"Under whose orders?"

"I'm with the DEVGRU SEAL unit and authorized by JSOC, which means I operate on direct orders from the president," said Luke. "Do you have a problem with that?"

A reluctant, crooked smile formed on the man's face as he glanced at Luke's uniform and then stood aside. "Be my guest," said the man. "You'll probably regret it anyway."

Luke watched as the man made his way to his two nearby companions and whispered something to them. They turned to look at Luke and it clearly wasn't a comforting look. It was the kind of look you give someone you suspect just stole your wallet. He observed quietly as they said something to the girl's mother. She looked upset by whatever they said. Then they turned and walked away. Something strange was going on here, but he wasn't sure what.

Luke turned as the young girl ran to him. She stopped just in front of him and smiled. He could tell at once her smile was warm and genuine. Her demeanor was miles away from the angry girl who challenged the strange visitor.

"I knew you'd come for me, Luke," she said.

"How did—"

Before he could continue to ask her how she knew his name, she hugged him. She seemed like a typical child, not one who could defy a deity. In fact, she reminded him quite a bit of Kayla. It's probably why he immediately liked her and felt intensely protective of her.

As he looked past her, he could see her mother approaching. Without a doubt, it was the same woman he'd seen with the girl on that fateful day at the church. She'd been wearing an Air Force uniform at the time. He could see now, she was tall, with long blond hair and deep blue, almond-shaped eyes like her daughter's. She had prominently high cheekbones and skin like porcelain. He'd barely noticed her that horrible day, but looking at her now, she was strikingly beautiful. She tapped her daughter on the shoulder.

"Ariella, I'm sure this man has more important things to do."

"It's quite alright," he said. "Actually, if you don't mind, I wanted to ask her a few questions. With your permission, of course."

"What kind of questions?" she replied, putting her hands on her hips.

"Easy ones, I promise. You can stay, of course."

"Oh, I'm not leaving her side, and like I told the others, if I don't like where this is headed, I'm pulling the plug. Got it?"

"I understand, Miss," said Luke. He admired her firm stance. She probably needed it trying to protect such a precocious daughter.

"It's Captain," she said. "Captain Cassandra Denton. I'm a staff psychologist with the Air Force Reserve. And you are?"

"It's okay, mom," said the girl. "This is Luke. I told you

we'd find him again."

The woman's eyes grew wide, and her body language softened. "This is Luke!? *Your* Luke?"

"*Her* Luke!?" said Luke. "Can someone explain to me what's going on here, and how you two know who I am?"

"You're Luke Remington," said the young girl, her expression growing more serious, "and you're supposed to help me."

"How the hell d—"

"Please excuse Ariella," said the woman. "She has kind of a sixth sense about things. I don't understand it myself. But she's been talking about you for years. Somehow, she knew something terrible would happen here today. And you're supposed to be a big part of the solution. That's all I know."

"Now, I'm even more confused than before," he said. "But I believe you. That's the problem." He knelt to be closer to Ariella's level. "Ariella, what exactly did you think would happen here today? What's my part in all this?"

"I don't know exactly," she said. "But I had one of my feelings that something bad was going to happen here. I knew someone was coming to visit us today. I knew it would be someone evil. He's not who he says he is." She paused and then looked into his eyes. "I also knew you would be here, Luke."

"How did you know?" he said.

"I just knew. So, I told my mom we had to come here today."

Luke looked up at Cassandra. "And you listened to her?" he said to her.

"You saw how it turned out," she said. "And her instincts haven't been wrong yet. They seem to be getting much more accurate and detailed as she gets older. So, yes, I trust whatever my daughter says."

Luke nodded. "Well, I can see why."

Luke couldn't describe it, but he felt a strange presence from her when he stood near Ariella—a certain calmness, yet a sense of intrinsic power. And the girl knew it.

"Ariella," he said, "you told the man he wasn't who he said he was, but that the true one would come for him. What exactly did you mean by that?"

"It's just a sense," said Ariella. "I... I get messages."

"What kind of messages? How?"

"In my head," she said. "I only know that the true protector will come and save us, and you're part of that, Luke."

"You must be confusing me with a holy man," said Luke. "That's not who I am anymore. I'm not sure I ever was."

"I know you've lost your faith. I understand. I'm sorry about your family. But this is bigger than you. It's bigger than all of us. You don't really have a choice."

He turned again to Cassandra. "How old is she?" he said.

"She's nine."

"More like nine going on thirty." He couldn't get over how eloquently she spoke for her age, not to mention the fact that she seemed to know everything about him, including what was in his head.

Ariella moved closer to him and said quietly, "Help me stop him, Luke. He's here to destroy our world, not save it."

"But what can I do?" he said. He couldn't believe he was asking this of a nine-year-old. "You saw what happened to all those people. By the way, what *did* happen to them, anyway?"

"I don't know for sure," she said. "But they're not alive. Not exactly. For now."

"Not exactly," he repeated, shaking his head. "For now? And you think I can help?"

"You have to trust me, Luke. I don't have all the answers now. But I will."

"Let's say I do try to help, whatever form that takes. Do we win?"

"I don't know," she said. "I only that that if you don't help, we'll lose."

Before Luke could say anything, his radio beeped.

"Excuse me," he said.

He picked up the radio. "Captain, sir."

"I've received orders from JSOC command," said Martinez. "All units are to stand down and return to base at Dam Neck. You joining us, Remington?"

"On my way, sir," replied Luke.

Luke was surprised they were being ordered back to Virginia Beach, but no doubt they'd be called upon to follow up.

"I've got to return to base," he said to Cassandra and Ariella. "How do I get in touch with you?"

"We'll be in touch with you," said Ariella. "You're about to go back on leave soon anyway."

Luke shook his head and laughed. "I'm not gonna ask how you knew I was supposed to be on leave, but we have a national emergency going on, so I doubt very much my leave will resume any time soon."

Ariella grinned as if she knew a secret he didn't. "You'll see, Luke. We'll see you in Philadelphia, sooner than you think."

"Just in case," said Cassandra, who appeared embarrassed, "here's my card." She handed him a card with a downtown Philadelphia address on Bainbridge Street.

"Philly?" he said. "I thought you're with the Air Force."

"I'm a member of the Reserve, but Ariella insisted I keep an office in Philadelphia. I'll give you three guesses why."

"Seems I have a guardian angel," he said.

"Contact me if you need," said Cassandra. "Otherwise, we'll find you."

Ariella stepped forward and gave Luke a hug.

Luke held her, marveling how she was at once an innocent

child with all the joy and warmth that went with it, and yet at the same time was extraordinarily powerful and intelligent, far beyond her years. Her gifts almost frightened him, but at least it seemed she was on his side.

As she left his heartfelt embrace, he stood and watched as she and her mother turned and walked away, disappearing into the crowd that was now being waved toward the parking garages. Part of him wanted to go with them and make sure they were safe, but he had his orders.

As he turned to head back to his team, he noticed the three men in black suits peering at Ariella and her mother as they walked away. The one Luke had spoken with, the one with the scar, turned toward him and stared.

Luke's instinct was usually right. Maybe not as right as Ariella's, but he had a pretty good track record himself, except for that one horrendous day. And this time, he was sensing something about these guys that didn't sit right. They knew more than they were letting on. He was sure of it. As he stared back at the scarred man, he felt the hairs on his neck tingling. And that was never a good sign.

CHAPTER 5

STAND DOWN

L uke had arrived back at the base in Dam Neck and was now in his quarters unwinding. As an E-6 Petty Officer, he'd been assigned to share his quarters with only one other SEAL, a Vietnamese guy named Li, but then Li decided to live off base with his fiancée, so Luke had the place to himself. Anyone E-5 and above, or even E-4 with at least four years of service, could live off base if they chose. Luke didn't really have ties anywhere these days, and he felt it would do well for his psyche to live on base for now, at least when he wasn't traveling.

He sat at his desk and tried to make sense of the day's events. Martinez had told him en route that a hotline had been established for families of those who'd vanished, and that the president would be holding a press conference later in the day. For now, the word would be that it was being investigated as a rogue terrorist event, with evidence of possible special effects used in the attack. Foreign governments have denied involvement. Of course, this was just the spin doctors at work to avoid public panic, but one more event like this would be all it would take to crack that fragile façade.

He had to admit, the alleged Jesus put on quite a convincing act. He almost would've bought it himself if it weren't for Ariella. The young girl mystified him even more than the false messiah. Assuming she was correct—and he wholeheartedly believed she was—then if this strange invader wasn't the true savior, then who or what *was* he? And why did he make his appearance at the same time as a terrorist attack—if that's even what it was? Were the events connected? Too much wasn't adding up. Then there were those men in black suits.

He thought again to Ariella and Cassandra. They seemed legitimate. Ariella certainly had an undeniable gift. He could attest to that simply by the things she knew about him that she couldn't have gotten from anywhere else. He always prided himself on being a good judge of character, and the two of them came across as completely sincere. So, here he was, somehow stuck between a nine-year-old girl and a Jesus imposter, both with otherworldly power. Of course, it could well be that they were both quite literally otherworldly, but his head was about to explode just thinking about it. He would have to gradually get to know Ariella and Cassandra and make his assessment. As for the mystical Jesus-wannabee, he hoped he'd never see him again. At this point, he wasn't even sure he'd want to meet the *real* one.

Frustrated with his lack of knowledge and the metaphysical elements at play, he decided to take a more grounded approach and study the video from his headset camera. His hand shaking slightly, he pulled out the camera module and connected it to the monitor in his kit with the supplied cable. Then he began watching.

He fast forwarded the clip until it got to the first explosion. He watched as the one news helicopter fired the rocket. Then the other. By the time the recording angle got back to ground level, the other black-clad terrorists had already left the news vans. By all accounts, this looked like a well-planned terrorist attack, nothing more—though it was still a mystery who these men were. But then everything was overshadowed by the immense, blinding flash that lit up the sky. He held his ears as the sound on the monitor vibrated from the low hum that he recalled being emitted by the bright light. What had caused that sound? He advanced the clip frame by frame.

At first it just looked like a white screen. This would've been when he shielded his eyes, but the camera had fortunately kept recording. As he clicked through the frames, he saw what appeared to be a fuzzy distortion in the sky, a blurred pattern across one of the clouds. He advanced the frames until it disappeared. He rewatched that portion of the clip several times, but he couldn't draw any conclusion from it. It was possible it was just a strange cloud pattern. Undoubtedly, others must've recorded the event from different angles, so perhaps someone else was able to pick up something he didn't.

As he advanced the clip, the bright light subdued, and the mysterious figure was already standing on the ground. Could it have been some high-tech magic? It was possible, but then that didn't explain Ariella. He fast-forwarded to the part where Ariella stepped forward. Everything was as he remembered it. Even the part where the figure and his followers vanished didn't reveal anything new.

He got up from his chair and then collapsed onto the bed exhausted. He figured he'd get some rest until Hawthorne's scheduled briefing this evening. He was curious to learn what the next course of action would be. Surely there'd have to be some targeted intelligence on the matter, and he assumed all military branches would be on red alert.

As tired as he was, his mind kept racing, but then eventually he gave in to the fatigue and started drifting off. He could've sworn he heard a voice say 'Listen,' but figured he must've imagined it. He tried to awaken but was too tired.

"*Listen*," said the voice once more, in a faraway whisper. A cold chill ran through his veins. It was the unmistakable voice of the deity who had appeared at the UN.

"*Do you not hear your wife and daughter calling to you?*" said the voice, much more clearly this time. "*Come join me. They're waiting for you.*"

"Lucas," said another voice from beyond. It was Kathleen's voice. "It wasn't your fault. Come with us."

"Come with us, Daddy," said the unmistakable voice of Kayla.

"Kayla!" he said. "Kathleen! Are you both okay!?"

A dark fog rose in front of him, and when it cleared he saw them both standing before him, half in silhouette. He missed them so much. He tried to reach out, but he was too weak, as if his hands weighed a hundred pounds.

"Come with us, Lucas," said Kathleen.

"I can't!" he yelled. "I want to, but I can't!"

"You can, Lucas. Just try."

He thought about the absurdity of the situation, Kathleen and Kayla calling for him to join them in the afterlife. Then he remembered the source of their visit, the untrustworthy savior, and he realized something. This had to be the cruelest of cruel jokes, a twisted mirage. Because, whoever or whatever was trying to lure him made one simple, but glaring, mistake.

"Get out of my head!" he yelled. "Ariella was right. You're not real! I swear, whatever it takes, I will kill you and send you back to whatever world you came from. Because any lord worth his salt would know that my wife never called me Lucas. Now, get out!"

"*Very well,*" said the voice of the false messiah. "*Your path is chosen.*"

Luke watched in horror as his flames engulfed his wife and daughter, their screams penetrating his soul.

A siren sounded. Was it a fire alarm?

He suddenly opened his eyes in a cold sweat and felt disoriented. The alarm was still humming. Then he realized. It wasn't a fire alarm. It was the fifteen-minute notification warning calling all personnel to Hawthorne's briefing. He looked around the room and nothing was disturbed. Was it all a dream? He sure hoped so. He could practically still smell the smoke from the flames. He wondered, was it his guilt over his inability to save Kathleen and Kayla, or was it his fear over whether he was making the right choice in believing Ariella? He just hoped it wasn't the entity trying to get inside his head. At any rate, he'd won that battle of wits. But he knew in his gut the war was just getting started.

He made his way to the shower and got ready to find out what their next course of action would be. He joined others from the unit as they made their way to the briefing, gossiping over what their orders would be, who the terrorists might have been, and what they thought really happened at the UN.

As Luke entered the conference hall and took a seat, he noticed Admiral Hargrove talking with a man in a black suit. Luke couldn't see the man's face, but from Hawthorne's animated gestures, it was obvious the deputy commander was challenging what he was being told. He wondered. That suit and that build looked familiar.

As the man in the black suit turned to leave, Luke's suspicions turned out to be correct. That scar was a telltale sign. He was one who'd confronted him at the UN. The man once again glared at Luke and flashed that crooked smile. Luke turned toward Hargrove and could tell he was miffed over whatever had been said. He watched, curious, as Hargrove stepped up to the podium.

"I'm going to keep this short and sweet," said Hargrove. "After a meeting between JSOC, the Joint Chiefs, and the president's Chief of Staff, I've just received word that all military branches have been ordered to stand down."

Luke couldn't believe what he was hearing, and from the looks of some of the other SEALs' faces, he wasn't alone in his assessment.

Hargrove continued. "I know this isn't what any of us were expecting, but the fact is this matter is now in the hands of the CIA and the Director of National Intelligence. They will be advising the president, the NSA, and Homeland Security. We will be informed of any change. Those of you who have family leave coming are to take it. You will all be on call until further notice. Dismissed." Hargrove turned abruptly and left the room.

Luke was flabbergasted, though he shouldn't have been surprised. Clearly there were government secrets at play here, and more than a little back-door politicking. Hargrove likely knew more than he was letting on and was probably just as incensed as he was. At any rate, for those with top-secret military clearance to be kept in the dark on such a high-profile event was infuriating.

It appeared he'd be going on leave after all. How did Ariella know? And what did those men in the black suits know about her—if anything? He had even more questions now than before, and if was going to get any answers, it would have to be from that unusual young girl. He took out Cassandra's card and looked at it. He was determined to get to the bottom of what was going on, and if it had to be through unofficial back channels, then so be it.

CHAPTER 6

SURPRISE GUEST

L The seven-hour bus ride from Virginia Beach to Philadelphia had gone by quickly, considering Luke had slept half the time. He wasn't sure what his plans would be, but he knew he wanted to visit his family, and he especially needed to meet with Cassandra and Ariella. He'd already left a voice message for Cassandra letting him know Ariella was right and that he was on leave.

The bus pulled into the terminal on Market Street and the doors opened with a hiss. After making way for an elderly woman who grabbed her bags and pushed through the aisle like a battering ram, Luke retrieved his duffel bag and got off. His dad had insisted on picking him up at the station, so Luke headed inside to meet him. As soon as he stepped through the doors, he spotted his father on a bench, and, surprisingly, a familiar face was next to him. A scarred face.

"Kevin?" said Luke. "I sure didn't expect to see you."

Kevin Royster smiled. "Welcome home Luke. It's a good surprise, I hope."

"Of course." He had to admit he was confused as he shook

Royster's hand.

"Welcome back, son," said his father, holding his arms out.

Luke turned to embrace his father, who appeared a bit preoccupied.

"Everything okay?" he said. "How's mom?"

"She's good. She'll be thrilled to see you. I heard through the grapevine you were at the UN during that nonsense."

"News travels fast," said Luke. "How did you—"

"We'll talk more in the car," said his father.

"I saw the TV report," added Royster. "What's your take on it?"

"Let's talk about it when we get out of the terminal," said Luke. As he followed his father and Royster to the car, he surveyed the area, just to be sure nobody was watching him. He was feeling more and more paranoid the last few days.

As soon as they got in the car, Royster didn't waste any time.

"So, what was it like there?" said Royster from the back seat. "What do you make of that little girl?"

"I know as much as you," said Luke.

"She was all over the news," said his father. "They didn't release her name, though, because she's a minor. Did you meet her?"

"Why would I have met her?" said Luke. "There were thousands of people there."

Royster leaned forward from the back. "We just thought—"

Luke's father held up his hand to interrupt Royster. "It's just that... the girl looked so innocent. But she stood up against what looked like... well, you know what it looked like, Luke. You were there. The thing is, who do you think was right?"

"That's the big question, isn't it?" said Luke.

"Yes," said his father. "It is. I know who your grandfather

believes."

"I can imagine," said Luke.

"He thinks the rapture's upon us. I personally have my doubts. But I'll tell you, I don't know what to think any more."

"That makes two of us," said Luke.

Out of the corner of his eye, he could see Royster shrug his shoulders in the back seat while his father looked in the rear-view mirror. Something was up between those two that they weren't saying.

"Well, the girl certainly looks innocent enough," said his father. "I'll give her that. I find this whole thing a bit ironic, though."

"How so?" said Luke.

"Well, with you trying so hard to leave Christ and all, and then lo and behold, Christ finds you."

Luke smiled, but he was too nervous about the situation to truly appreciate the humor. Instead, he changed the subject.

"So, what brings you here, Kevin?" he said.

"Well, to be honest, I heard from my military friends you were going on leave, so I checked in with your parents, and here I am!"

"Well, I'm glad to see you."

Something in Royster's voice sounded off. Like he was nervous.

They were all pretty much silent the rest of the way, and then as they pulled onto his parents' street, Luke couldn't believe his eyes. There were swarms of press outside his house.

"What the—"

"It's okay," said his father. "I can explain. The truth is, I asked Kevin to join me to pick you up. I thought maybe you'd tell him what you might not tell me."

"What are you talking about?" said Luke. "Tell you what?"

Just as they arrived at the house, three police vehicles pulled up. Brody jumped out from the front vehicle and ordered his men to move out the crowd of reporters.

"Your mother must've called the police to get all those reporters out of here," said his father.

"Why are they here?"

"Just come in the house, Luke. I'll explain."

Luke got out of the car and followed his father and Royster inside the house.

As soon as he entered the living room, his mouth dropped.

His mother was sitting in an armchair, and opposite her on the couch sat Cassandra and Ariella.

"Oh good," said Ariella, turning toward him with a slight smile. "You're back."

◆

At least Luke understood now why his father and Royster were asking so many questions about her.

"You better hear what she has to say, Luke," said his father.

Ariella stood up and stepped forward.

"We need to go to the Fox Chase Cancer Center, Luke."

"Who has cancer?"

"The false one will be there in one hour," she said, matter-of-factly. "He will be there to save people. He will not be saving them, Luke. We have to stop him."

Just then, there was a rapid knock on the door, and then it opened. Brody entered and said, "We're trying to get them cleared out, and—"

Then his face turned white as he saw Ariella.

"Her!" he said.

"Lieutenant, it's not what you think," said Luke. "She's helping us. I don't have time to explain, but can you get us an escort to the Fox Chase Cancer Center? It's urgent and we can't afford any delay. I'll explain when we get there."

"If you say so, Reverend," he said. "Consider it done."

Luke didn't bother telling Brody that he no longer needed to call him Reverend.

"Give me and my men a few minutes to clear a path," said Brody as he headed for the door. "As soon as I blare the siren, come on outside."

Cassandra approached Luke. Every time he saw her, he couldn't help but admire her radiant face and her captivating eyes, and he felt guilty for it every time.

"I tried to tell her we shouldn't come to your family's house," she said. "But you know how she gets."

"It's okay," said Luke. "I only have about a million questions for you later."

"I may not have a million answers," she said.

"Right now, I just have one. Why here?"

"I told you," she said. "Ariella insisted."

"No, I mean why would this… thing… pick a hospital an hour from where we are. Out of all the places in the world."

"Because he knows where I am," interjected Ariella. "And he knows you're here, too."

"Well, that's not creepy at all," he said. "And you think we should go where he wants… why?"

"Because we have to," she said.

"That's what I used to tell my kid," he said.

"Ariella," said Cassandra. "*How* does he know?"

Ariella shook her head. "I don't know," she said. "I only sense it."

Luke looked at Cassandra, who shrugged her shoulders.

Just then, they heard the blip of Brody's siren.

"Time to go," said Luke.

"I'm going with you," said his father.

"No, I don't want you involved in this any more than you are already."

"It wasn't a question, Luke. I want to know what's going on, here."

"I'm coming, too," said Royster. "For extra support."

"They can help," said Ariella. "But we have to go now."

Luke shook his head and then acquiesced. "Okay, well let's get going then."

He couldn't imagine what awaited them at the hospital, and he didn't relish the thought of seeing that all-powerful entity again, whatever it was. And now he finds out they're all probably walking into a trap.

CHAPTER 7

MIRACLE AT FOX CHASE

L uke sat in the passenger side next to Cassandra, who'd offered to drive. What would have been well over an hour ride to the Fox Chase Cancer Center took less than forty-five minutes with the police escort. As they pulled into the hospital parking lot, Luke watched in horror as a brilliant, bright light flashed in the sky, just as it did during the encounter at the United Nations. The low-pitched hum rattled the car windows.

"He's here," said Ariella from the back. "We have to hurry." The poor girl was wedged in the middle between Luke's father and Kevin Royster.

Finally, Cassandra pulled in front of the entrance.

"You may want to get out here," she said.

Brody pulled beside them and lowered his window.

"Me and my men will secure the area while you guys head inside," he said.

Luke and the others left Cassandra's car and headed inside.

As soon as they entered through the sliding glass doors, he could see that the guards seemed to be in some kind of trance.

"That's not a good sign," said Royster.

They proceeded past the administration desk. The women at the desk seemed to be just standing and staring up the corridor.

"This way," said Ariella, leading Luke and the others up the right corridor toward the first-floor patient rooms.

Up ahead, Luke could see the flowing white robe of what, for all intents and purposes, looked like Jesus. A doctor and a nurse were walking beside him, seemingly pleading with him to leave.

Just then, a well-dressed woman came out of one of the rooms who seemed surprised to see Luke and company.

"Pastor Remington!" she said. "I'm surprised to see—"

"Not now," said Luke and his father in unison.

She huffed as they proceeded past her, just as the robed figure stopped in front of a CAT Scan sign. Two orderlies were wheeling a female patient in as the large double doors to the scanning area opened automatically.

A few more nurses and visitors gathered to watch the strange sight of a robed Jesus in the hospital corridor. There was a certain glow about him Luke couldn't quite identify— barely visible, but it was there, making him look even more ethereal.

Luke watched as the mysterious entity stepped into the CAT Scan area and turned to face the gathering crowd, raising his draped arms to speak.

"Kevin, can you record this?" said Luke.

Royster took out his mobile phone and began recording.

"Behold," said the crisp, clear voice that rang through the hallway. "The woman that lies here is riddled with illness. She has but months to add to her life." He walked to the head of the gurney she was lying on and put his hand on her shoulder. "Yet, I will add many years," he said, smiling, "and ultimately, an eternity."

The robed savior raised his arms to the ceiling and immediately a bright glow surrounded the woman. The lighting in the corridor flickered on and off and the equipment in the CAT Scan room began shaking.

Luke shielded his eyes as the glowing light intensified. He could feel the hairs on his arms tingling. He glanced down at Ariella, whose long hair was standing straight up. The loud hum had returned.

Then, as quickly as it started, everything went silent. The light faded and all was back to normal—except for the fact that the messianic visitor was still standing in the CAT Scan entranceway.

"It is done," said the entity, lowering his arms. "This woman… and all those in this infirmary…" He looked around and then continued. "… no longer carry the vile ailment that had consumed their bodies."

Luke glanced over to make sure Royster was still recording, which he was. Then he turned to see one of the doctors checking the CAT scan to make sure it was still operational. After powering it up, the doctor motioned to the nurse to have the patient scanned.

"I'm going to check out the patient myself, if you don't mind," said the doctor.

The entity turned and smiled. "If it eases your doubt," he said, reassuringly, "your machine will bear witness to the miracle performed here today."

Luke looked at Ariella just in time to see her abruptly step forward. He was afraid this would happen. He spotted Cassandra, who had just arrived, and she just shrugged her shoulders as if this was perfectly routine.

"Why cure them?" said Ariella, loudly enough for everyone to hear.

Luke was wondering the same thing. It occurred to him

that either this was truly Christ, and he was backing the wrong horse in Ariella, or it was something else entirely, possibly fatting the pigs for slaughter.

"Child," said the entity, with a twinkling glimpse of recognition. "Where is your mercy?"

"I meant why now?" she said. "You're going to take them all anyway."

Ariella moved closer to the messianic figure, stopping just a few feet in front of him. "Besides," she added, "you're not doing this for mercy. Are you?"

"Don't listen to her!" yelled a heavy-set thirty-ish woman standing outside one of the patient rooms. "She's a nonbeliever!"

The entity put up his hand. "Have mercy on those who doubt," he said, glancing around at the awestruck gatherers. "For soon they shall see. But know this. Blessed are those who have *not* seen and yet still believe."

"But I *have* seen," said Ariella.

The entity's eyes narrowed. "Bear not false witness, child. Turn from your ways and cast the demon from your soul." His eyes began to glow.

Just then, Luke jumped forward and stood between Ariella and the imposing figure. Though he hadn't been able to protect his own daughter, he sure wasn't going to make that mistake with Ariella.

"I think what she's trying to say," said Luke, "is that she believes you're... a wolf... in shepherd's clothing."

"And the wolf," said the entity, staring calmly at Luke, "shall dwell with the lamb, and the leopard shall lie down with the young goat." His voice grew louder as he looked around and continued. "And the calf," he bellowed, "and the young lion and the fatling together." He held out his robed arms and smiled, victorious in his answer, as if revealing some great revelation.

"And a little child shall lead them," said Luke, glancing down at Ariella. "I know my Isaiah."

"A child indeed," said the entity, gazing down at Ariella, who had snuck up beside Luke. Then he paused and leaned in toward Luke. "But is she?" he said in a near whisper.

On instinct, Luke put his arm around her. His head was so mixed up, he didn't know what to believe anymore.

"The time has come," said the entity, turning to the crowd, "for me to visit the multitudes and purge their ailments as I have done this day. More infirmaries await, and disease and pestilence reign free. But hear my word, brethren. The righteous among you shall spread news of my coming, and in seven days I shall call upon you. And on that day, those who come may rejoice in my kingdom."

"And what of those who don't?" said Ariella.

"All must make their choice," said the entity as he walked back up the corridor toward the exit.

Just then, a patient came running out of his room behind Luke, his nurse chasing after him nervously.

"I feel better!" said the patient. "It's like a switch went off! I can walk!"

"That's Mr. Dempsey!" said one of the other nurses. "That's impossible!"

It was mass chaos in the halls, and just as Luke looked toward the exit, he saw a bright light envelope the robed entity. The light was blinding, and within seconds it began to fade. When Luke's vision cleared, the figure was gone.

Luke turned around just in time to see the doctor from earlier re-emerge from out of the CAT Scan area, holding a report. The puzzled physician seemed to be half in a daze.

"It's unbelievable," said the doctor. "It's truly a miracle."

"It's not a miracle," said Ariella. "He wants you to believe it is. But it's just technology."

"Then how do you explain that this woman had a stage

four glioblastoma and now it's gone?" The doctor spoke to Ariella as if she were an adult. "No technology can do that."

"I don't need to explain it," she said. "Just because you don't understand something doesn't mean it's a miracle. It means it's advanced science, novel radiotherapies and immunotherapies you haven't yet encountered. Or more likely nanotechnology-based solar molecular targeting. Based on the light, of course."

The doctor looked at her, then at Luke. "Who *is* this girl?" he said.

"Don't ask," said Luke, as he pulled Ariella away.

As he tried to lead Ariella and his group toward the exit to reconvene outside, other confused nurses started coming into the corridor and telling the doctor their patients' symptoms had miraculously vanished.

Before long, Luke and his group had exited the hospital, where Brody was with several other police officers trying to corral people who were coming in and out of the hospital, as well as the masses gathering in the parking lot. People were standing outside their cars staring at the sky, as news of the bright flash must've spread.

Luke turned to his father as Cassandra and Ariella walked ahead of them. "What did you make of that?" he said.

"I'm not entirely sure, to be honest. It sure looked like a miracle. But something about that girl…"

Luke nodded.

"I don't know what to think," said Royster.

"That reminds me," said Luke. "Can you send me the footage you took?"

"Sure thing, Reverend."

"Just Luke is fine."

Cassandra and Ariella waited outside the car for Luke and the others. Just as he approached them, Brody came running over.

"What the hell happened in there?" said the out-of-breath police officer.

"The second coming," said Luke. "It looks like there'll be a lot more."

"Luke," said his father, "you're gonna feel awfully bad if he turns out to be the real thing."

"Don't worry," said Ariella. "He isn't."

Luke's father knelt at her level. "But couldn't a miracle really happen?"

"Miracles happen every day," she said. "This wasn't one of them."

"Well, we'll find that out one way or another," said Brody. "We have video of those skies and we're gonna review them back at the station. I'll let you know if we find anything unusual."

"Unusual," echoed Luke, laughing. As if everything so far hadn't been completely bizarre.

"Well, more unusual than all this," said Brody, waving his arm around. "By the way, please tell me you got video from inside."

"I have it right here in my phone," said Royster. "I can send it to you."

"Good, do that," said Brody.

After Brody headed off, they piled into Cassandra's car. Just as he got in the passenger seat, Luke spotted a black sedan pulling into the parking lot. The windshields were dark, and it had government license plates. Two men in black suits exited the vehicle and rushed inside the front door. He recognized one of them as the scarred man who'd confronted him at the UN, and who'd later given Hargrove the orders to stand down.

"I don't trust them," said Ariella from the back seat.

Luke turned around to see her staring out the window at the black sedan.

"That makes two of us," he said.

"Bad things are going to happen, Luke," she said. "Very bad things."

"What's going to happen?"

She didn't respond.

"What's going to happen, Ariella?" he repeated.

"I don't know exactly," she said. "But you need to be careful."

CHAPTER 8

ANSWERS

As they approached his parents' house, Luke was surprised there were no reporters waiting outside. Then again, they probably had all left to cover the hospital situation. Needless to say, when he checked his phone, the number one trending topic was #JesusIsBack followed closely by #PhillyMiracle. Word traveled fast. Cassandra pulled up to the driveway and his father and Royster got out. She had generously offered to drop Luke off at his house afterward.

"It must be tough going back to your house," said Cassandra, as she drove off. "If you ever need to talk, I'm here. I mean I *am* a psychologist."

"I appreciate that," said Luke. "But I'm okay for now."

"He's being polite," said Ariella.

"Ariella," said Cassandra, "you know what's not polite? Commenting on people's personal thoughts."

"I'm just saying," said Ariella.

Luke couldn't help but laugh.

"She's quite an impressive girl," he said.

"You haven't seen anything," said Cassandra. "But yeah.

She's pretty amazing."

Luke tried to imagine Ariella in classes with other kids her age.

"Is she in school?" he asked.

"Sort of. She's always been different than other kids. Started talking at six months old, walking at nine months. She could read by the time she was three. As for school, let's just say we've had a few talks about keeping her thoughts to herself."

"So, what do you mean 'sort of?'"

"Hello?" said Ariella from the back seat. "I'm right here. And to answer your question, I'm home schooled now. The advanced classes were too primitive anyway."

Cassandra blushed. "Sometimes, it's easy to forget she's a kid."

For the first time in years, Luke actually felt some type of bond with a woman other than his wife. Cassandra looked to be in her early thirties, about his age. He could tell she was a good person; he had a sense about people. And he could also tell Ariella's spirit was in the right place. But there was so much more to learn about them both.

His mind drifted and he started thinking about all those witnesses to the mystical, robed figure's arrival, and the ones who were taken. They wanted so much to believe. They *needed* to believe. And in some ways, he did, too, if only so someone up there could explain why bad things happen to good people. But every fiber in his being told him that this wasn't the real deal—that these *miracles* had an ulterior, sinister purpose. Ariella certainly sensed it. And she'd been right about everything so far.

As they approached Luke's house, all the memories of the past came flooding back. He was having second thoughts about going in and decided that after they'd left, he'd drive to a motel for the night.

"Luke," said Ariella, "I know you don't want to go in. We have an apartment available above Mommy's office."

"Ariella!" said Cassandra.

"No, it's okay," he said. He looked over at Cassandra. "Don't worry, I know how kids are."

"No, she's right," said Cassandra. "We do have an apartment available. I just didn't want her to blurt out everything she senses. The truth is, we would both love for you to check it out. It would be a nice break for you. But Luke, before you make any drastic changes, you need time to grieve."

"It's been three years," he said. "You know, this is the first time I've been back here since. I joined the SEALs right after it happened. I thought it might be different by now. But…"

"You're still in trauma, Luke. You never gave yourself time to grieve. You jumped right into the fire after you lost your whole world. Why don't you come back with us? You can look at the apartment, and you can tell me all about that family of yours."

"He's experiencing guilt, too," said Ariella. "Luke, it wasn't your fault."

"Ariella, shush!" said Cassandra. "Sorry," she said to Luke. "Junior psychologist in training."

Luke smiled and nodded. "No, she's right. As usual. You know what? If that offer still stands, I'll take you up on it."

"Of course, it stands," said Cassandra. "Do you want to follow us?"

"Sure thing," said Luke. "And thanks to you both."

As Luke exited the car, he heard Ariella say to her mother, "I told you he'd be coming to our house."

◆

Luke had parked in the small lot on Bainbridge that Cassandra had told him about. The colonial brownstones were in the heart of the historic district and had to be going for at least a million. As he left his car and made his way to her address on the left, Cassandra and Ariella were waiting outside. When he greeted them, he noticed the simple, white sign posted on a blue door that said, *Cassandra Denton, PhD – Licensed Psychologist*. An unmarked brown door with a keypad was just to the right of it.

"This door leads to the apartments," said Cassandra as she entered a code into the keypad and opened the door.

"Short commute to work," he said.

"I spend a week out of every month at the Dover Air Force Base, but otherwise I can't complain," she said, as they ascended the wooden stairs to the apartment on the second floor.

When they got to the apartment, Cassandra unlocked the door and he followed them inside.

The living room was surprisingly modern and spacious, with hardwood floors and a large bookcase with everything from literary novels to art books to psychology and military tomes. At the center of the room was a light grey fabric sofa and two matching armchairs, all stuffed with cozy, matching grey and white pillows. A pile of travel books sat atop a small glass coffee table. Kathleen would've loved this place.

"Can I get you anything?" said Cassandra. "Coffee? Tea?"

"Coffee would be nice," he said.

"He takes it black, with one teaspoon of sugar," said Ariella.

"Ariella!" said Cassandra.

"Well, he does."

"So, you can read minds *and* tell the future?" said Luke. He had to admit, it was starting to make him a bit uneasy.

"Well, not exactly," said Ariella. "I just sense things. But the longer I'm around someone, the more I feel it."

"Can you control it?"

"Not really. Feelings just come to me. Places, names, events. Sometimes I don't know the context until it happens. But it always happens."

"Like I said, she's getting more accurate the older she gets," said Cassandra as she waited for the water to boil. "Pretty much everything she's said has come true."

"Well, I can tell you one thing," said Luke. "She's the first nine-year-old I've seen that knows the word *context*." He turned to Ariella. "So, do you know what I'm going to have for breakfast tomorrow?"

"First of all, no," said Ariella. "Second, if I told you, you could decide to eat something else."

"So, your visions aren't a foregone conclusion."

"Not always," she said.

"I like to call them snapshots of a possible future," said Cassandra, as she poured the boiling water into the French press coffee maker. "When she was younger, I thought she had hyper-empathy syndrome, but then I saw it went beyond that. I have to say, I'm not a big believer in parapsychology, but when I see the things Ariella can do, I start to wonder."

"I helped my mom avoid a car accident, once," said Ariella.

"Wow," said Luke. "How did you manage that?"

"It's what she does," said Cassandra as she brought Luke his cup of coffee. The aroma of the dark roast smelled incredible, and it occurred to him he'd have to get a French press. "Ariella kept insisting I switch lanes, and sure enough a tractor trailer came barreling out of control from the oncoming lane into the lane I was just in."

"That's one special little girl," said Luke, sipping his coffee.

"Mommy, let's show him the apartment now!" said Ariella, changing gears and suddenly sounding like a regular nine-year-old.

"I have a better idea," said Cassandra. "Why don't you say goodnight to Luke and get ready for bed and I'll show him the apartment? It's almost ten o'clock."

"What you really mean," said Ariella, "is that you want to talk to Luke without me around. You do know I'm not a little girl anymore and you can talk in front of me. But I understand."

She gave her mom a kiss and hugged Luke, who held the coffee mug out so as not to spill it on her.

"Goodnight, Luke," said Ariella. "I'll see you tomorrow."

"You sure will," he said. She'd given in astonishingly easily, more so than most kids her age when it came to bedtime. He marveled at the job Cassandra had done being a single parent of such a special child and keeping a psychology practice on top of it, not to mention her Air Force Reserve work. He wasn't sure who impressed him more, Ariella or Cassandra.

After he finished his coffee, Cassandra led him out of the apartment, locking the door behind her.

"It's a two-bedroom, just like mine," she said. "I own the whole building. I didn't feel like paying rent and not having anything to show for it. My dad left me some money when he passed, so that helped."

"Sorry about your dad," he said.

"It was five years ago. But it still feels like yesterday."

"I can relate."

"Oh, of course," she said. "I'm sorry. I—"

"It's okay," he said. "As I used to say to my congregation, there's no monopoly on grief. My loss doesn't make yours any less painful."

He followed her to the third-floor apartment and watched as she unlocked the door. Frankly, he didn't even care about where he lived, but it was a good opportunity to learn more about Cassandra and Ariella. Though he had to admit, living upstairs from them wouldn't be a bad idea.

"Cassandra—"

"Call me Cass, by the way," she said as they entered the

vacant apartment. The living room looked even more spacious without all the furniture. To his right, he noticed the same counter as in the downstairs apartment, which separated the kitchen from the main room.

"Okay," he said, leaning against the counter. "Cass it is. What exactly happened with Ariella and school?"

"It's a bit of a long story," she said. "But the gist of it is, people started taking notice of her, and the more intelligence she showed, the more questions I started getting from the teachers. It got to the point where the other students would pick on her. But what started as a social issue became much more after the Gifford explosion."

"The Gifford explosion? You mean the elementary school? What happened? I heard miraculously nobody was hurt."

"Well, it was no miracle. It was Ariella."

"I thought the explosion was due to a natural gas leak or something."

"It was. I meant it was Ariella who saved all the students. Apparently, she got one of her feelings that something bad was going to happen. She asked her teacher to be excused, and then went into the hallway and activated the fire alarm. She was only seven then. She had to use a chair to reach it. Can you believe that?"

"With her, I can believe anything."

"Anyway, the alarm sounded, and within minutes, the whole school was evacuated. Ariella already knew the schoolyard location for her class to line up outside for fire drills and was already there waiting when the rest of her class got there. She told me what happened as soon as I picked her up, but I told her to keep quiet about it. Everyone was safe, that's all that mattered."

"I can see why you pulled her out of school, though."

"Actually, it wasn't that," said Cassandra. "The next day, two federal agents showed up at my office. They said the security monitors picked up Ariella sounding the alarm before the explosion, so they wanted to talk to her. The school was closed for repairs, so she was home that day. Let's just say it was quite the inquisition—and that was only the first of a whole string of visits. They wanted to run tests and I kept refusing."

"What made them give up?"

"Who says they gave up? I did manage to get a lawyer I know to get them to ease up on the pestering and that helped for a while. But that incident at the UN kickstarted things all over again. Now they won't leave us alone."

Luke thought back to the men in the black suits who were questioning Cassandra back at the UN. This explained a lot. But not everything.

"I hate to ask this," said Luke. "But what about Ariella's father? Where's he in all this?"

He couldn't quite read the expression on her face, but the look was enough to make him sorry he asked.

"How about if I show you the apartment first?" she said, clearly trying to avoid the subject.

"Of course," said Luke. "I'd like to see it."

He followed her as she led him past the kitchen to the hallway where the two bedrooms were, their footsteps echoing on the hardwood floors. The rooms were deceptively large, as was the whole apartment. His mind going in a million directions, so he was barely processing what she was telling him about the history of the house, which dated back to 1870.

"I thought he was the one," she suddenly blurted out.

"Who?"

"Gideon Hain. Ariella's father. I was twenty-three and I was in Israel for my master's thesis on Kahneman and Tversky. They were basically the Lennon and McCartney of social science, and Israel's always been at the forefront of military psychology. Back in the days of Benny Shalit, they were the first to embed field psychologists in army units. Anyway, I was interviewing Israeli pilots out in the field when I noticed a handsome man in a grey suit watching. He was standing with the staff sergeant. Next thing I knew, the staff sergeant brought him over and suggested I meet with the guy."

"And that was Gideon?"

"Yep. Turns out he was some kind of military advisor. Not only was he giving the sergeant tips on combat readiness, but when I met with him he had some really good insights around human psychology and decision-making. The predictability of fallacies in judgement during stress, and things like that. I won't bore you with the details. I'll just say it went beyond anything I learned in school. He must've asked me a million questions, too. He was one of those guys who seemed to know everything about everything. You know the type."

"I sure do."

"Except he wasn't a know-it-all, he was humble. Anyway, you can see where this is leading. We got to know each other. The more we spoke, the more fascinated I became with this brilliant and kind man. I mean, he was smart, but you could tell he genuinely cared about people. At least I thought so at the time. We spent one night together in my hotel room. He had to leave in the morning for an appointment. We were supposed to meet later in the day, but now that I think about it, I should have known something was up. Even the way he said goodbye. It was warm, but it sounded so final." Her mind drifted for a few seconds, then she continued. "Six weeks later, I was back in the states when I found out I was pregnant."

"I guess you were surprised," said Luke.

"Shocked is more like it. I was on birth control, and he was the only one I'd been with in months. Sorry if it's TMI, but the point is, there was no way I should've been pregnant."

"I assume you tried to look him up again."

"I tried for months. I even had one of my Air Force

contacts who's pretty high up do some digging. There was no record of a Gideon Hain in the Israeli military, the Mossad, or any other source he looked up, either in Israel or the states. Whoever he was, he was well hidden and off the books. So, either he was the world's biggest jerk, which I have a hard time believing, or he was something else entirely."

Luke was as baffled as she was by the bizarre mystery. But she had to be thinking what he was thinking. "You don't think he had Ariella's gifts, do you?"

"I don't know what to think. Maybe he did. Maybe something happened to him. Or maybe the government got ahold of him like they tried to with Ariella. But when you add everything together—Ariella, her father's disappearance, my miracle pregnancy—it all seems so strange."

"And getting stranger by the day."

He could see her eyes welling up as her mind drifted. He felt bad for bringing the subject up to begin with.

"Cass," he said, "you don't have to do this all alone anymore. I promise I'll help see this through. I won't abandon you, don't worry."

"I'm okay, really," she said, composing herself. "I can handle this."

"I know you can. You've done amazing so far, more than anyone could. But now none of us can handle this alone. We're a team now, right?" He held her arm gently and then let go. He wasn't sure if he let go because of his own guilt or that he didn't want to seem too presumptuous. At any rate, he couldn't deny he felt a close connection to her.

She smiled and nodded. "Damn right we are."

He couldn't get over her strength of spirit. He meant what he said. Not many people would have the fortitude to hold it together and achieve all she has while taking care of an enigmatic child like Ariella.

He glanced at his watch, an old Tissot his father had given

him when he became a pastor, with the words *Get me to the church on time* engraved on the back with his initials. "I suppose I better let you get to bed," he said.

"But we never got to talk about you and your family," she said. "I'm supposed to be helping you, not the other way around."

"You did help me," he said. "Believe me, I appreciated the company. Besides, it's more for us to talk about next time."

"Well, I do have appointments in the morning. But we can visit you around four thirty if that works. My last appointment's at three."

"I have a better idea. Why don't I take you and Ariella to dinner? Dante and Luigi's in South Philly. I'll share what I learned from the recordings, and then we can plan our next steps."

Her face turned pale.

"Look, if you don't like Italian—"

"No, it's not that," she said. "It's just that Ariella said you were going to invite us to dinner tomorrow."

"Well, she *has* been known to be correct on occasion."

"That's the problem. She said she had a weird feeling we wouldn't be going, but that's all she could see. Something about a change of plans. And she seemed really worried."

CHAPTER 9

REVIEW

L uke pulled up in front of his parents' house. It was ten in the morning, and he noticed Lieutenant Brody's car was already parked across the street. He'd spent the night on the couch in his living room, but otherwise he'd slept surprisingly soundly—and later than usual. As he walked up the concrete steps to their front door, he could hear his father, Kevin Royster, and Brody all talking in animated fashion. As soon as he opened the door, his father called out to him.

"Luke," he said. "Come here. I'd like to see what you make of this."

They were watching a video on the TV. Judging by the wires that were spread out on the floor, someone must've connected Brody's dashcam to the television with an HDMI cable.

"I'm gonna rewind it and play it again," said Brody. "Keep an eye above the hospital at the top of the screen when the sky lights up."

Luke sat on the couch and focused intently on the screen. He was pretty sure he knew what Brody was talking about. When the bright light appeared, he noticed the distortion immediately.

"That's exactly the same anomaly I noticed in my helmet-cam footage when he appeared at the UN," he said. "I thought maybe it was from the intensity of the light, or even heat distortion, but that doesn't quite explain it. At any rate, my footage got confiscated by—"

"I'm not done yet," said Brody. "I took it to our lab and had them do their magic to enhance it. Now I'm gonna play the cleaned-up version and pay attention to the same area."

Brody inserted a micro-SD card into the player and pressed play. This time, only the sky was on the screen, and when the light flashed, several separate distortions could be seen, like transparent, glistening ovals that reflected off the clouds. Brody paused the image and turned to Luke.

"Look at that," said Brody. "Four distinct oval shapes that are exactly the same size, spaced evenly apart. There's no way that's a coincidence or an optical illusion. I'm telling you there's something there. And if you—"

Several loud bangs on the front door interrupted his sentence and made Luke practically jump out of his seat. Whoever it was, they were frantic and kept pounding on the door. Luke jumped up and ran to door and looked through the peephole. Then he opened the door.

It was Cassandra and Ariella.

"You need to destroy the footage you have," said Ariella before he could even ask what was up.

"Quick, you need to do it now!" she shouted.

"I'm sorry," said Cassandra. "But you better listen to her. She woke up screaming and said if we didn't get over here fast, you were all in danger. She even said..." her voice cut off as she got choked up.

"Said what?" said Luke.

"She said some of you would be killed if we don't act fast."

"I need that SD card," said Luke to Brody.

"But—"

"Hurry!" said Ariella.

"No time to explain," said Luke, looking at Brody. "Trust me."

Brody took the card out of the dashcam and hesitatingly held it out.

Luke grabbed it, ran into the bathroom, and flushed it down the toilet.

Brody looked at him incredulously as he returned from the bathroom.

"You better have a damn good reason for—"

Just then, another loud bang on the front door shook everyone to their core. Then the door came bursting open and armed men in black suits rushed in and ordered everyone to get down on the floor.

Luke complied, as did the others.

"Search the house," said a voice from the door. As the man entered, Luke spotted the scar immediately. It was the same guy from the UN and the base. Luke was glad his mother was visiting cousins for the day. She'd be terrified.

"Who the hell are you guys," said Brody, still kneeling on the floor. "I'm Lieutenant Brody with the Philadelphia Police." He reached for his badge.

"We know who you are, Brody," said the scarred man. We know all of you. And right now, you're going to tell me where that footage is."

"What footage?" said Luke.

"Oh, we're not going to play that game, are we?"

"It's over there," said Brody, pointing to the dashcam. "But there's nothing special on it, so you have nothing to worry about."

Brody was smart to point them to the raw, unenhanced footage. He must've popped the original card back in before the men entered. Now to see if they'd buy it.

Luke watched as the scar-faced man walked to the dashcam and picked it up. He played the footage on the TV. When it ended, he stood there, seemingly contemplating what he'd seen. He took a deep breath, then played it again. After it ended, he stood there thinking some more, and then played it again a third time, pausing at various spots. Then he popped out the card.

"Take this with you," he said to one of his men. Then he walked toward Luke and the others and faced them.

"Did any of you spot anything unusual on that recording?"

Luke shook his head, as did Brody and the others.

"I'm gonna ask this a different way. My name is Special Agent Kilgore. I'm with a branch of the Central Intelligence Agency that handles, shall we say, less mainstream activities of national importance. And we have an issue of *tremendous* national importance happening right now. You don't need me to tell you that. Now, if anyone here noticed anything unusual, keeping that from us not only is stupid, but it could be seen as interfering with national security. So, I'll ask one last time. Has anyone here seen anything you wish to point out to us?"

Luke wasn't sure what to think, but he trusted Ariella more than anyone, and if she said these guys were no good, he was inclined to believe her.

"If we saw anything, we'd tell you," said Luke. "We were trying to make sense of the situation, like everyone else. But we didn't see anything. I can promise you that."

Kilgore stared at him as if he wasn't buying any of it. "Promises, promises," he said. Then he nodded.

"Very well," he said. "You *were* a reverend, so I'll give you credit for that. Sorry about the wife and kid, by the way."

"You can take the dashcam card if you want," said Brody. "It's no good to us."

"Oh, we will," said Kilgore.

"Special Agent Kilgore," said Luke. He knew there was a

risk to asking this, but he needed to know who these guys were.

Kilgore turned toward him.

"How do we know you're really with the CIA? I mean for all we know, you could be with some foreign government. After all, we *all* want to protect national security."

Kilgore gave that crooked smile of his. "Of course, Petty Officer Remington. I would expect nothing less from a member of our illustrious SEALs." Kilgore flashed a legitimate-looking CIA badge that said *Lance Kilgore*, and below the name was a bar code and his title, *Senior Special Agent*.

"Satisfied?" he said.

Luke nodded.

Kilgore showed the badge to Luke's father, Royster, and Brody, for some reason skipping Cassandra and Ariella.

"I'm only going to say this one time and one time only," said Kilgore to the group. "This is a matter of national security, and we need you all to back off. All military has been ordered to stand down, and that also goes for local police, former pastors, and special little girls who don't know when to be quiet." He looked at Ariella, who was kneeling on the ground like the others. "The president himself and his top advisors have decided to let what is transpiring run its course."

"Its course?" said Luke. "How do we know what its course is?"

Kilgore glared at him. "There are parties that are privy to information that you are not. So, I'll put it in plain, unambiguous terms. If anyone here interferes with the natural course of events, you'll be charged with treason and be dealt with accordingly. Do I make myself clear?"

Luke nodded.

"I need all of you to acknowledge that you heard."

"We heard," said Brody, and the others followed suit.

Kilgore nodded and waved his men out the door. He went

to follow them, but then stopped in his tracks. Slowly, he turned and stepped toward Cassandra and Ariella.

"You know, you have the biggest challenge of all," he said to Cassandra. "Keeping that daughter of yours in check and all. For everyone's safety, see to it that you do. We wouldn't want anything to happen to her. Or you."

"They'll be fine," said Luke, standing up. "We heard your rules, Kilgore. You can stop short of threatening little girls."

"Are you challenging my authority?" said Kilgore approaching Luke. "You have no idea what you're dealing with."

Before Luke could answer, he noticed Ariella get up out of the corner of his eye. Kilgore noticed it too.

Ariella walked over to the scar-faced man and looked up at him. She had that determined look on her face, like she had when she confronted the robed entity. But this time, Luke could *feel* it. He was almost certain the temperature in the room had just dropped. For the first time, Kilgore had an expression of concern on his face.

"I would be very, very careful who you threaten, Special Agent Kilgore," she said. "Others have threatened me and my family…and my friends….and you *know* what happened to them. Besides, I wouldn't want your son James to come to any harm."

Kilgore's eyes widened. But he didn't reply. He just stared at her for a moment. Without saying a word, he turned and looked back at Luke and then walked toward the door to join his men.

◆

"Does somebody want to tell me what the hell is going on?" said Brody as they all got to their feet.

Luke tried to lock the door after the men had left, but the

lock was busted.

"You'll need a locksmith for that," he said to his father.

"Anyone?" said Brody. "Because I don't know what the hell I just witnessed."

"I think Luke can explain," said Luke's dad. "Can't you, Luke?"

"I'm completely confused now," said Royster.

Ariella stepped forward.

"They were looking for the recording you took," she said, looking at Brody. "And if they found the other version or if they believed you knew something, they would have had all of you locked up. And a few of you would have disappeared for good."

"Wait a minute," said Brody, staring at Luke in shock. "How in God's name does she know about the other version?"

"I'm not sure God has anything to do with it," said Ariella.

"It's a figure of speech, kid, but—"

"Why didn't they know about *my* recording?" said Royster.

"They did know," said Ariella. "They just didn't care. Because you didn't record what Lieutenant Brody did. Their secret."

"What secret?" said Luke.

"Something they don't want you to know about. Something in the sky. That's all I can see for now. Something really bad is coming, Luke. I can feel it."

"How does she know all this!?" shouted Brody, clearly growing more frustrated by the minute.

"Guys," said Royster. "Is anyone else curious about why Ariella spooked Kilgore? Or is it just me?"

"Kevin has a point," said Luke, looking over at Cassandra and Ariella. "Is there something else you two aren't telling us? I think it's safe to say we're all in this together now."

Cassandra looked at Ariella and nodded. Ariella looked

hesitant to speak, but then she got up the courage.

"I have visions sometimes," she said, which Luke felt was the understatement of the century. "Most of you have seen that already. But when the government found out about me, they started harassing my mom. One time they took her and left me home alone with three guards. They just wanted to question her, but I didn't know that. So, I made the guards have some accidents."

"What, do you mean… like peeing accidents?" said Brody.

"No, more like accidents with their guns," she said matter-of-factly, as if she were talking about bubblegum flavors. "Anyway, one got hurt more than I expected, and he was in a coma for a month."

"And how are you not locked up in juvie?" said Brody.

"I was only six," said Ariella. "And he shot himself."

"Only six," he muttered to himself. "I'm a year from retirement and this is what I'm dealing with."

"So, this guy Kilgore must've heard about that and got spooked," said Luke. "Well, that would definitely explain his reaction."

"Special Agent Kilgore," said Ariella, "was the one in the coma. I guess you noticed his scar."

Luke wasn't sure whether to laugh or be terrified. He looked at the others, who appeared equally shocked.

"Ariella has much better control of her emotions now," said Cassandra. "I gave her some tools that help."

"I didn't mean to hurt him," said Ariella. "Not really."

"It's okay, dear," said Luke's father, bending down and putting a hand on her shoulder. "Anyone here would've done the same if we could. We'd do anything to protect our families."

"I know I would've," said Luke.

"And you're absolutely sure," said Brody to Ariella, "that this Jesus isn't the real deal. I mean maybe those things in the sky were invisible chariots or something."

Ariella shook her head. "Oh no, they weren't... chariots," she said in a whimsical tone that made chills run down Luke's spine.

"Listen, everyone," said Luke. "I've seen about ten instances so far where Ariella's been absolutely correct. It's clear the government knows more than they're letting on—they so much as said so. Now, I may not have special powers like she does, but something tells me this is going to get a lot worse before it gets better, and Ariella is the key to finding out the truth. Until she gives us reason not to, I say we have to trust what she says."

"I'm with Luke on this," said Luke's father.

"Me too," said Royster.

Brody scratched his chin. "You do realize," he said, "the kind of danger we could all be in if we press on here. I don't have jurisdiction when it comes to national security."

"I understand completely if you don't want to take part in this. That goes for any of you. I intend to get to the bottom of what's happening here."

"Take part in what, exactly?" said Brody. "Do you have a plan?"

"Well, we'll need to be covert about it. We'll need burner phones. We'll have to meet in public places. I may need you as lookouts. We may have to do more. We may need more allies. But until I meet with Admiral Wilcox and see if he knows why the military was told to stand down, I don't have enough information for a plan. He's a family friend and is pretty high up."

"So, you don't have a plan and you're just playing this one step at a time."

"Pretty much," said Luke.

"Okay, I'm in."

"You are?" said Luke. He certainly wasn't expecting that

answer.

"Sure. Haste makes waste. Besides, who needs retirement?"

Luke wasn't sure if he was being sarcastic or not, but he was glad for the help.

"I'm in too," said Royster. "Heck, I wouldn't be alive if it wasn't for you."

"And you know I'm in," said Luke's father.

"Great," said Luke. "I'll meet with Admiral Wilcox and get the phones. I'll be in touch, and we can take it from there. Is that—"

"Above all else..." said Ariella. Everyone turned and listened intently to the girl whose presence commanded the room. "... I need you all to believe me and do the things I ask, no matter how crazy it may seem. I may need us to do some things you may not like. Things that may be scary. In fact, I sense we'll definitely have to do some really scary things. Things I don't want to do, but we have to. I didn't ask to get all these weird messages in my head, but I have them and I think we need to follow them. So, no matter what all of you may think, if I say we need to do something, we have to do it. The false one is even stronger than me and he means to hurt everyone. I don't know who he is yet or whether we can even stop him, but we have to try. Besides, we need to stop him or else we..." Her voice tailed off.

"Or else what?" said Brody.

"Or else a lot of people will be dead."

"What do you mean a lot?" said Luke.

"A lot," she repeated. "So, are you all going to believe me if I say we need to do something?"

They all appeared dumbfounded as the little nine-year-old put her hands on her hips.

Brody spoke first.

"Sounds like we don't have a choice," he said. "Unless you

ask us to kidnap a kangaroo or something."

"You got us this far," said Luke. "I say let's see how this goes."

"Good," she said. "Now, we have a problem we have to talk about."

"What is it?"

"The men who were here. How did they know you'd all be here reviewing the footage?"

Luke thought about it and immediately he could feel the hairs on his arms stand up. "Could they have followed you?"

"It's not likely," she said. "How would they know about your recordings?"

"Dammit, she's right," said Brody. "We have to check for bugs."

"If they were bugging the room," said Luke, "they'd know everything we were saying. They'd have been back here already. And if they were bugging you, they'd have known about the enhanced footage."

"I'm afraid it's something much worse," said Ariella. "They have help."

CHAPTER 10

NEW ASSIGNMENT

Special Agent Lance Kilgore had a unique set of skills and he knew it. Having started at MIT in the *Computation and Cognition* program, he ended up getting involved in PoET, their *Program on Emerging Technologies*, where he focused on the global impact of subjects as diverse as genetic engineering, nanotech, biotech, and more. From genetically tailored CRISPr babies in China to other applications of synthetic biology and genomics—especially in military circles—he had special interest in how these paradigm shifters could impact societies, cultures, and policies, not to mention the geopolitical implications. Before he knew it, he'd been recruited into the CIA, which unbeknownst to him, had financed MIT's Center for International Studies, of which his program was part.

After joining the CIA, he'd been given a special assignment abroad, traveling from Eastern Europe to China under the auspices of consulting to research organizations, but which secretly involved espionage and obtainment of emerging tech. The inherent danger required him to undergo training as an operative, which he adapted to more easily than he—or anyone—had expected. Perhaps it was because he came from a long line of cops, not to mention his background in martial arts. At any rate, it came in handy in one close call incident in Moscow.

Part scientist, part commando, he soon became a coveted asset, sought after by foreign agents but always remaining loyal to the CIA. His focus was on anything that would benefit his country and give them an advantage. And so, it was with special interest that he approached a new assignment back in the states—finding out what he could about the little girl who'd saved all the kids in her elementary school by clearing the school out before the event happened. But he quickly learned—firsthand—how dangerous she truly was. That whole period was a blur. He recalled the helpless feeling as his own gun had lifted toward his face.

After he'd recovered, he became even more intent on getting to the bottom of her skills. It was personal now. Come hell or high water, he was going to tap into those talents. Above all, he needed to prevent her from falling into the hands of a foreign government, but also, he couldn't ignore the tremendous potential to harness that ability for the US. But now, everything had changed. The cat was out of the bag with the girl, but that was the least of his problems. Now, there was a new player involved—a player with even more powerful gifts, and who was more cooperative. But it came with strings attached. Heavy strings.

Kilgore parked his black sedan in front of the CIA safe house, an old farmhouse out in Yardley that looked more like it should be selling fresh eggs. The other agents were already there. As soon as he stepped out of the car, he felt that horrible tingle in his body. It was as if he had no control over his limbs or organs—a godawful weightless feeling. Then he heard that confounded hum.

In an instant, a bright light flooded his eyes as he gave into the feeling. When his vision cleared, he was no longer beside his car. He was back in *that* place.

He turned around and the glowing robed figure was right behind him.

"Jesus Christ, you scared the hell out of me!" he said.

Seamlessly, the figure transformed into a dapper, seventy-something man in a grey suit.

"Perhaps this is more to your liking?" said the man, who still had a certain glow about him. The man's voice had a metallic echo.

Kilgore glanced out the window and saw nothing but black space and stars. The Earth was far below. All he could do was thank the Lord for artificial gravity. Still, he felt queasy. Having your molecules disassembled and reassembled will do that.

"I don't care what form you take," he said. "Just give me a little warning next time."

"Are the data farms ready?" said the man.

"Of course. We did everything you asked."

"Good. The incident will occur in four days' time." He always referred to it as the *incident*. "And the location?"

"Death Valley," said Kilgore. "It's in the northern Mojave Desert. It meets all your criteria."

"Then the word will be spread."

"It's already begun," said Kilgore. "How do we know you'll hold up your end of the bargain?"

"Human lives for technology is a bargain indeed. Do not worry. You will have your machinery and your bioforms. You can resume your petty little wars once we get the bodies we need. But there is one more matter to discuss."

"You mean the girl."

"You've taken great pains to fulfill our plans. She could interrupt them. See to it that she does not."

"I've warned her," said Kilgore. "She'll listen this time."

"She will not. Even now, she plants seeds of rebellion. I

sense her. She is different from humans, and yet… not. Something about her is… familiar."

"Familiar, how?"

"In ways only I can see. But it is of no consequence."

"I don't understand."

"You must go," said the entity, ignoring his line of inquiry. "Remember, from seeds grow infestations. You must pluck it out at the root."

"You mean kill her."

"And her companions. Do you object to this course of action?"

Kilgore shook his head. "Not at all."

"Then I have chosen correctly," said the entity. "Soon you shall be rewarded. But if you fail… if this young child should by some means interrupt the pilgrimage—the rapture, if you will—then I need not remind you that we will not stop with Death Valley." He practically spat out the last two words with venom.

"The rapture will happen," said Kilgore.

So, he had his assignment now. He'd done worse. Hundreds of thousands of people would soon disappear. What was a few more? It would be a shame to waste the girl's talents, but he'd soon have access to all the biotechnology he'd need. He'd be responsible for the greatest advancements in military history the world has ever known. Still, he couldn't help but wonder why the girl was so familiar to this unearthly being. As far as he knew, she was clairvoyant with powers of telekinesis. Now he was wondering if she was perhaps something else.

CHAPTER 11

CHECKING IN

Luke was getting frustrated. He'd made numerous calls to
Admiral Wilcox's office, but every time he'd called, the
admiral was either on another line or had stepped out of
the office. It had been over three hours, and now the
receptionist was telling him the admiral was out for the rest of
the day. He had a feeling he was getting the runaround, but he
didn't expect it from Wilcox.

"I can leave a note for him if you wish," she said. "He'll be
back tomorrow."

"Yes, please tell him it's urgent." What he really wanted to
say was that they could all be dead by tomorrow.

When he hung up the phone he was startled by a knock on
the front door. He slowly walked to the door and peered out
the peephole. The mailman was standing there holding a letter.
At least he hoped it was the mailman. He didn't recognize him.

Luke grabbed a weapon and opened the door slowly, just
in case.

"Can I help you?" he said, keeping the pistol hidden.

"Yeah, I got a letter here that requires your signature," said the mailman, a portly guy with red hair. The man held out a form for Luke to sign.

Luke looked at the letter and found it odd that there was no stamp on it. Plus, the envelope was blank. He gripped his weapon behind him and glanced around to see if anyone else was there. Aside from one of his neighbors who was working on the garden, he didn't see anyone or anything unusual.

"The envelope's blank," said Luke. "Who sent this?"

"A secret admirer," said the mailman.

Luke stared at the guy and then noticed the mail truck parked across the street. So, the guy really was a mailman. Either that or he went to great lengths to look like one. Luke signed the form and then took the letter from the mailman's outstretched hand. He watched with puzzlement as the mailman walked back to his mail truck. What kind of mailman delivers a blank envelope with a signature required?

As soon as he went back inside and opened the envelope, Luke knew who it was from immediately. The letter was brief to the point.

1700 hours at the site we used to meet post LL. Come alone. Wilco.

It wasn't hard to figure out. Wilco was not only the typical military acknowledgment that one *will comply* with orders, but it also happened to be the nickname his grandfather had given Admiral Wilcox. LL no doubt was referring to Luke's Little League games as a kid. After each game, Wilcox used to meet Luke and his grandfather at Pat's Steaks.

He looked at his watch. It was almost four o'clock. Hurriedly, he grabbed his keys and rushed out the door. It was rush hour, so it would probably take him about thirty to forty minutes to get there. Plus, he wanted to make a few stops along the way, just to be sure he wasn't being followed.

As soon as he got outside, he looked around for any suspicious parked vehicles. Satisfied he wasn't being watched, he climbed into his car and drove to a gas station to fuel up. Still wary of his surroundings, he then proceeded to a pharmacy and went inside, where he wandered around the store and picked up a few random items: a bottle of water, a small bag of pistachios, and a chocolate bar. Then he noticed the rack of prepaid phone cards. He grabbed ten of them, just in case. After one more stop to pick up burner phones for the cards, he headed toward South Philly. He switched lanes a few times to be sure he wasn't being followed, and even exited I-95 early and pulled back onto the highway at the next entrance.

At four-fifty, he was finally pulling into a parking spot on Ninth Street. He exited the car and walked across the street to Pat's. He could already smell the steaks and onions on the grill, and the faint whiff of Cheez Whiz. There was a huge line, which itself brought back memories. He loved coming here as a child. His dad generally didn't come because he was working. He remembered his grandfather and one of the other Little League parents used to debate about who made better steak sandwiches, Pat's or Geno's. His grandfather used to argue that it wasn't a real Philly cheesesteak unless the meat was chopped like Pat's. Geno's used thicker, sliced strips, which a number of the other parents preferred. Luke always liked them both equally, to his grandfather's dismay.

As he stood in line he heard his name being called. Standing a few feet to his left was Admiral Wilcox, wearing a Phillies cap and a tan suede bomber jacket. Luke didn't recognize him at first because he was in civilian clothes.

"Admiral," said Luke. "I didn't see you there."

Wilcox held up a brown paper bag.

"Already got your steak," said the admiral. "Provolone with fried onions and sauce. That's your MO if I recall."

Luke laughed. "You have a good memory."

"Don't worry. I won't tell your grandfather you didn't get Cheez Whiz."

Luke followed him to the outdoor countertop, where they stood and unwrapped their cheesesteaks.

"So, what exactly is going on, Admiral?" said Luke. "We're getting visits from this… I don't know what… with ungodly powers, pardon the pun, claiming to be Christ. The military's been ordered to stand down. That Kilgore character from the CIA is involved somehow. I've had a couple run-ins with him already."

"Oh, I know all about your run-ins," said Wilcox. "You've been traveling with that girl."

"Ariella," said Luke. "She has some kind of psychic ability. I still don't understand it all, but she senses something's up with this Kilgore and I believe her. And she sees right through this messiah business. What do you know about her?"

"That's the problem," said the admiral. "Her file's locked tighter than Fort Knox. It's classified above my level."

Luke was stunned by the admiral's words. "Above your level? You're commander of the entire Navy SEAL operations."

"Luke, here's the deal," said the admiral. "My official orders were to stand down. But I also received some top-secret secondary orders, and that's what has me worried."

"Secondary orders, sir?"

The admiral leaned in closer. "There's something coming, Luke. Something big. I don't know where or when, but I was told it's a matter of days. I was told to be prepared to have our men gear up the day *after* this mysterious event." He paused briefly. "Meanwhile, our fearless leaders are telling citizens to make their own choices and to do as their beliefs tell them. If that's the case, then what is it exactly I'm being asked to prepare for?"

"Have they given you any hints?"

"Only to stay on base and keep quiet. Clearly, they know something, but the politicians are playing this close to the vest, from the president on down."

"That's disturbing."

"That's not the disturbing part. What's disturbing is the reason I asked you to meet me."

"There's something else?"

"Luke, I have a few friends on the inside in the White House. They don't know much, other than that there's a lot of frantic, hush hush talk that indicates the administration is covering something up. Aside from that, they're more in the dark than I am. But one of them did hear something. Something about you."

"Me?"

"I won't beat around the bush. You, the girl, and her mother are being put on a watch list. Which makes it all the more difficult what I'm going to ask you to do."

"What do you need me to do?"

"Disappear. All three of you. I don't know what's going to go down at this event, but once it's announced, I have a feeling we'll all know about it. Once we do, you'll need to get the girl there, because if her file is locked down that tight and the three of you are being watched, then they're afraid of something. And that's a good thing, because she may be our only hope of finding out what's really going on and maybe stopping it if we have to."

"We already planned to find out what we could, so I guess this is what we have to do."

"Who's *we?*"

"Well, now it'll just be Cassandra, Ariella, and me. Originally, Lieutenant Brody, my old Navy friend Kevin Royster, and my dad offered to help."

"Do me a favor," said the admiral. "Leave your dad home. I can protect your family, but I can't protect you. Plus, I have an idea this could get dicey."

"Don't worry, Admiral. I wouldn't put anyone in danger that doesn't have to be."

"Good. Remember, you have to protect that girl at all costs. Do you have a place to go? Somewhere you don't have to register your name?"

Luke thought about it for a moment.

"My in-laws have a cabin in the Poconos. They were always trying to get Kathleen and me to stay there."

"I suggest you go there in the next couple days. Take the girl and her mother, and make sure you're not followed. Check under your vehicle for trackers. Remember your SERE training. You'll need all those evasion techniques."

Luke thought back to the grueling SERE training. SERE stood for Survival, Evasion, Resistance, and Escape. He could never forget the grueling ordeal spent in the rugged mountains of Maine and the hot Southern California desert, meant to emulate enemy territory. It was more intense than he could've imagined, and the evasion program involved traveling from safe house to safe house via heavily patrolled routes.

"I'll talk to your family about laying low in the meantime," said the admiral. "As far as everyone knows, you just disappeared. Anything through official channels should be considered a threat. And of course, the usual, no cell phones, no credit cards."

"Of course."

"There's going to be a special public statement tonight from the president. I'm not privy to what's going to be said exactly, but expect something along the lines of don't panic, things are still being assessed, talks are in progress, blah blah blah. You were right to trust the girl. She'll be your best bet to find out what's really going on."

"I can't tell you how much I appreciate your help," said Luke.

"Don't get too excited, because it's the last time I can help you. After today, you can't call me or come to my office. You're on your own from here, so be careful. If I can find a way to reach you, I will, but don't count on it."

"Copy that, Admiral," said Luke.

"And if anyone else in your party decides to join you, make sure they know it's at their own risk."

Luke thought about it. He couldn't expect Brody or Kevin Royster to put their lives on the line. Especially after what Kevin had been through.

"I can't ask them to join me on this," he said.

The admiral saluted Luke and they finished eating their cheesesteaks.

"I'll tell you one thing," said Wilcox. "That's a damn good steak. Same as always. Oh, by the way, there *is* one more thing. It's important."

"There's something else?"

"Yes. You were a reverend before you were a SEAL. You have a day or two before you have to be gone from here. Take a few minutes in the morning and go to the church."

"I haven't been back there in—"

"That's okay. Go. Pray a little. You'll need it. We all will."

CHAPTER 12

SUNDAY SERVICE

Luke stood outside the door of Saint George's Church, hesitant to go in. It had been over two and a half years since he'd last stepped foot inside the place where his life had changed so drastically in a matter of seconds. At least it was two hours before the first service, so thankfully nobody would be there at this hour except for his father and grandfather. Still, it was hard to shake the memories. He took a deep breath, trying to suppress the awful visions that kept popping into his head.

Mustering the strength, he opened the pair of stained-oak double doors, which squealed with the sound of dusty hinges. Just then, his grandfather came storming out of his father's office to the right, muttering under his breath. His grandfather barely acknowledged him as he whizzed by him and left the church in a huff.

Luke headed to his father's office. He could see his father in the open doorway, sitting at his mahogany desk.

"What was that all about?" he said as he approached the office.

"Oh, Luke," said his father, standing to greet him. His father waved him in as if there was some big secret to tell, even though they were the only ones in the two-hundred-year-old building. Luke stepped into the office, observing the pale-yellow paint that was peeling off the walls.

"Did you meet with the admiral yet?" said his father.

"You first, Dad. What were you two arguing about?"

"Oh, you know. Your grandfather thinks the rapture is coming. I guess you saw the news about that."

"You mean about the social media posts?"

"Yeah, they're all saying there's some big event on the fifth in Death Valley. They're calling all Christians to come to a happening. That's what they called it on the news, a *happening*."

"I saw that," said Luke. "That's three days from now."

His father took a seat at his desk.

"Everyone's convinced it's the end of times," said the elder Pastor Remington. "Between the political upheaval, the natural disasters, and the diseases going around, I can't say I blame them for believing it."

"That's exactly why we have to warn everyone."

"There's some people, if they don't know, you can't tell 'em. I forget who said that."

"It was Yogi Berra," said Luke.

"What I'd like to know is where this Death Valley location came from. Who started the rumor?"

"That's suspicious in itself." Luke took a seat opposite him.

"I always say, Luke, all this social media stuff has made the world a lot smaller, which is a wonderful thing, but it also gave the Devil his biggest weapon. Unfortunately, your grandfather fell for it, hook, line, and sinker. I told him to look up Matthew 24:24."

He passed an open Bible across the desk. Luke took it and read the passage out loud.

"For false messiahs and false prophets will appear and

perform great signs and wonders to deceive, if possible, even the elect."

Luke closed the Bible and handed it back to his father. "That's truer than you realize."

His father leaned forward. "What is it, Luke? What did Wilcox say?"

Luke didn't know where to begin. "I assume you saw the president's address last night."

"Sure. It wasn't a very revealing one. He pretty much said to follow your beliefs, and then spent most of the time rambling on about religious freedoms and all that. What did you think he'd say?"

"I didn't expect anything different, I suppose. Dad, would you say the president is a religious man?"

"Well, he claims to be a devout Christian. Goes to church every Sunday with his family and all that. Why?"

"I'm wondering why he made a special point about how he's duty-bound to remain in the White House. He made it pretty clear he wouldn't be attending the event. He didn't even seem the least bit conflicted about it."

"Such is the burden of leadership."

"According to Wilcox, there's a different reason. He said the president's speech would be a cover-up. He didn't know all the details, but he said he was told to be prepared for the day after a mysterious, upcoming event. And this was before it got spread on social media, so the president knew about this Death Valley event beforehand."

"Think the government's in on this?"

"Not only that, but I'd bet anything they were the ones who spread the rumors about Death Valley in the first place. Anyway, Wilcox suggested I disappear for a while with Ariella and Cassandra so we can piece all this together. I'll need to get Ariella to this event somehow. We may need her to confront this... whatever he is."

Luke picked up a "Grandpa rocks" stone paperweight on his father desk, which was much heavier than he remembered. He'd bought that for his father as a gift from Kayla before he went off to Afghanistan.

"Wait a minute," said his father. "I thought we were all in this together."

"I can't put any of you through that risk," he said, putting the stone paperweight back on the desk.

"But where will you go?"

"For your own safety, I can't tell you that, Dad. The admiral said he can help protect you and Mom, but I'll need to hide out with Ariella and Cassandra until we figure out the next steps."

"At least take Lieutenant Brody and Kevin. You'll need all the help you can get."

"I can't ask them to get involved."

"Luke, they insisted on being a part of this."

"Things have changed." He couldn't in good conscience put Brody and Royster in harm's way.

"Listen, I'll do my part here. If I have to warn congregants about the risk of false prophets, I will. But at least give Brody and Kevin the chance to say no."

Luke thought about it, and then nodded.

Just then, Luke heard the creaky front door open.

"Expecting anyone?" he said.

"Not this early, but—"

"Luke," called a familiar voice from the church lobby. It was Ariella.

He and his father left the office and entered the lobby just as Ariella and Cassandra came rushing up.

"She insisted we come," said Cassandra. "I had to cancel my appointments. I think she—"

"Someone's coming, Luke," said Ariella. "They've been tracking me. I can sense it."

"Who? Who's been tracking you?"

She shook her head. "I don't know, I just feel it. And they're coming here." A sudden realization hit her face as she put her hand to her mouth. "I shouldn't be here. I think I led them to you. We have to leave."

"But I can't leave," said Luke's father. "I have a service coming up."

As they stood debating what to do, the church doors started to move slightly.

"We can't waste time," said Luke. "There's a side door up front."

As the doors began to open slowly, their creaky hinges sounding like they were about to fall off, Ariella held up her hand and turned to Luke.

"Wait," she said. "This is something different. Something bigger."

"Is that supposed to make me feel better?" he said.

The doors opened further, allowing glistening beams of natural sunlight to flood the church, making it practically impossible to see who was entering. Luke could hear a single pair of footsteps but could only make out the silhouette of a figure. Then his vision adjusted, and he could see the visitor's face. It was a dark-haired man with greying temples who appeared to be in his forties or fifties. He appeared to be of Middle Eastern descent. The man was carrying a small, black case in his left hand and wore a charcoal grey suit.

"You've been following me," said Ariella, matter-of-factly.

"I knew your father," said the man. "And the An'za never lies." He smiled. "You *are* his daughter." He had a slight accent. It sounded Israeli.

"The An'za?" said Luke. "Who's the An'za?"

"The An'za is not a who," said the man. "It's what I hold in my hands." He held up the small case in his left hand and beamed as if it held a precious diamond worth millions. "It is how I have found the young lady I seek." He stepped forward and bent down toward Ariella.

"Careful," said Luke.

Ariella tensed up.

"My name is Elli," he said. "Elli Hassan. I bring a gift to you from your father."

"From Gideon!?" said Cassandra. "Is he alive?"

"I am quite sorry, I do not know," he said as he stood. "Allow me to explain. I am a Katsa with the Mossad." Luke wasn't familiar with the term, but he knew all about the Mossad.

As if he'd read Luke's mind, he glanced at Luke. "It is not unlike the field agents in your Central Intelligence Agency."

"For our sake," said Luke, "I hope it's not like the ones we've had to deal with."

"I assure you, Pastor Remington. Or should I say Petty Officer Remington. I am not like Mr. Kilgore." Luke was surprised the man knew his name, but if he was with the Mossad, he probably knew a lot more than that.

"You know Kilgore?" said Cassandra.

"It is my business to know. Yet I cannot interfere. But now? Now, I *must* interfere."

"Interfere how?" said Luke.

"Twelve years ago," said Elli, "I was introduced to a special man by my good friend, whom I will call Yitzhak, God rest his soul. Yitzhak was retired, but he served for decades in Unit 81. Unit 81 is... well, it is about as secretive as your Area 51. Yitzhak told me this man was a top advisor with the Weizmann Institute and suggested we meet. His name was Gideon Hain. Or so I was told."

"Gideon never told me about his job," said Cassandra.

"I can assure you," said Elli, "Gideon Hain was not with the Weizmann Institute. But... he was the wisest man I have ever met, and we became friends over the next two years. He was of great assistance, at least while he was… well, I cannot tell you how much he has helped advance our science, especially in the field of aviation. But alas, that wasn't his primary interest."

"What was his interest?" said Cassandra.

"In a word? You."

"Me!?" she said. "Is that why he left me high and dry to raise Ariella on my own?"

He smiled and shook his head. "All will become clear," he said. He reached into his jacket pocket and took out what looked like a quarter, except it was flat, with no markings on it whatsoever.

"What kind of coin is that?" said Ariella.

"It is not a coin, my dear," said Elli. He looked toward Luke and his father. "Would you be so kind as to lock the doors to your church?" he said. "I believe you have an hour yet before your service."

"You're quite well informed," said Luke's father, "Mr. Al… er El…"

"Elli Hassan. My full name is Eliezer."

"I'll get the doors," said Luke. He wondered if it was such a good idea, but this Elli Hassan guy seemed decent enough. Besides, Ariella was the best judge of character he knew. If she wasn't alarmed, then neither was he. Still, just to be sure, he glanced back at Ariella and she nodded.

Once the doors were locked and Luke returned, Elli held out the coin-like object in his open hand. Immediately, a pale blue light emanated from it and formed a large oval shape about six feet tall. Luke heard a low vibrational sound that wasn't too different from the sound made when the messianic imposter had arrived. Then the sound stopped, and, where the oval shape had been, a man appeared out of thin air—a tall, slender man with handsome features and dark hair. He looked to be around forty and was wearing a silver and blue uniform.

Luke couldn't place it.

"Gideon!" said Cassandra.

"It's my father!" said Ariella. Then her excitement waned. "But it's just a recording."

"A recording?" said Luke.

"That's impossible," said his father. "He's standing right there."

"The child is correct," said Elli. "Now, please observe."

CHAPTER 13

THE AN'ZA

Luke watched in awe as Gideon Hain slowly stepped toward them. It was as if he were in the room with them—not a hologram, but a true physical presence. Even his footsteps echoed somehow on the old wooden floors. Then he stopped.

"My name is Kersius," he said, in perfect English. "To you, I appear human, but in truth, I'm a scientist from a human-like race called the Alaktians. I realize this may be quite a shock to you. Our planet, Alaktu, is 4.2 light years from here—that's 6,300 of your Earth years—orbiting a star you call Proxima Centauri. In galactic terms, we're practically neighbors."

He smiled a warm smile. Luke wasn't sure if the being was trying to appear human or actually looked like that. But then he remembered how Gideon appeared to Cassandra—quite human, not to mention that if this being was instead green and had three heads, Ariella would've ended up looking quite different.

"Your planet is no stranger to my people," he continued. "Others from my world—along with less hospitable races—have come for centuries in search of *Kusi'ga* because it fuels their energy. You call it gold. But I came in search of something much more valuable."

Luke watched as the humanoid man called Kersius produced a bright blue stone from a shiny, black holster on his uniform and held it out for display.

"This is *An'za*. The word roughly means spirit stone. In fact, my people taught this word to your ancients thousands of years ago when we first discovered the stones here on this planet. Your people rediscovered it only recently, embedded in volcanic rocks near Mount Carmel in the land of Israel. You've come to call them Carmel Sapphires. To you, they are rare gems that fell from the sky, mysterious and harder than diamond. But to us, An'za is life itself. Through history, it could only be found three places—your world, my world, and in the endless cosmos. You see, our two worlds are far more special than you realize. Both our worlds have been coveted across the universe for our resources."

Luke looked around at the others, who were standing mesmerized as the man Cassandra formerly knew as Gideon put the glowing blue gem away in his holster. Luke had a million questions for Elli, but they would have to wait.

"By the time you see this transmission," continued Kersius, whose face grew more serious, "I may be long gone. It is my duty to tell you that our world has been decimated by a barbarous and deadly scavenger race called the Karn. Yours may be next. The Karn are led by an unrelenting tyrant who's terrorized galaxies far and wide. Our people call him Valdok the Destroyer. He's been known by many names among your ancestors. Abaddon. Apollyon. By any name, he brings chaos, death, and destruction, often in the guise of a false savior."

Luke and Cassandra looked at each other with wide eyes.

"It is in this spirit that I first came to your planet in search of An'za, which had long been depleted on our world. You may be wondering what this substance has to do with Valdok."

Kersius took what appeared to be a small, silver necklace out of his holster.

"With this modest, but magnificent stone," he said, "in combination with materials from my planet, I was able to generate a powerful talisman, strong enough to magnify our lifeforce a hundredfold. The hope was that its wearer could use its powers and help us stand even a small chance of defending our people. Alas, when I wore the talisman myself, it did not work. Our biology was too advanced to absorb the properties."

He held his head down in frustration and then looked up again.

"Humans are a primitive species," he continued. "Take no offense. By that, I mean your brains and biological systems are more malleable. Your race is twenty thousand years of evolution behind ours. But in this case, it is your strength. If our race was too evolved to adapt to my technology, yours would be quite suitable. I was certain of it. Fortunately, on a cellular level, we're quite similar. From my research, I knew without a doubt that if I mated with a human, our offspring would be superior and could one day harness even greater power from the An'za. But my chosen mate couldn't be just any human. It had to be someone with the wisdom and fortitude to raise what would no doubt be a very special and spirited child—a child that would one day benefit from the An'za and possibly help save what's left of your people and mine."

Cassandra turned to Luke and gave him a knowing look. He knew exactly what she was thinking. She'd been hand-picked by Kersius to bear his child.

"Cassandra," said Kersius, who was looking straight ahead, not at Cassandra, "my instructions were to deliver this message to you and to our child. Yes, I knew before I left that you were with child. But understand that I did only what was required to save our people. In doing so, it just may save yours. My instructions were to deliver this message to you and our child when he or she has reached the age of fifteen years. That is when the talisman stands the optimal chance of having its full effect. If you are receiving this earlier, sadly it means that Valdok has already arrived on Earth. My trusted friend Eliezer Hassan can explain the rest."

Luke watched as Kersius turned slightly, this time in Ariella's general direction, which may have been by coincidence. "And now, to my offspring, blood of my blood. May you be a beacon of hope for all worlds. May the An'za bring you strength, and may you be a leader of your people. Know that I will be with you always. For now, I must go help what remains of my people to fight our own battle with Valdok. It is likely too late for us. But in you, there is hope for the future."

With that, Kersius looked up and then vanished into thin air. Immediately, Elli put the coin-like object back in his pocket.

"I know you must be terribly confused," said Elli, looking at Cassandra.

"At least this explains why Gideon asked me so many questions when we met," she said.

Elli smiled. "I have watched your progress over the years with great interest." He looked at Ariella. "And you as well. Your father would have been very proud."

"Thank you," said Ariella, as if he'd offered her a lollipop. She seemed surprisingly calm at receiving such mind-boggling news. Cassandra put an arm around her.

"There have been but three people on Earth aware of Kersius and his message," said Elli. "There were three of us in case anything happened to me. And now, all of you know this great secret." He looked at Luke and his father. "I have done my research. I know you have proven to be faithful allies to

Ariella. I trust you will remain so."

"Of course," said Luke.

"Always," said his father.

Elli nodded. He held up the black case he was carrying and opened it. Inside was a sapphire-blue amulet on a silver necklace just like the one Kersius had held in the recording.

"As Kersius told you, I was asked to give this to the child of Cassandra when he or she reached the age of fifteen. But there was one exception. I was to act sooner if I saw certain signs. As you have been witnessing in your country, that time has now come. There is no question. The talisman may not work to full effect, but for all of our sakes, I hope it's enough."

"So, the necklace," said Luke. "That's the talisman?" He couldn't imagine all that power from one little stone.

"It is. With it, only a human with the blood of Alaktu can receive its properties. As Kersius explained it to me, it can unlock the potential of the spirit to gain mastery over energy, matter, wave forms, and much more. How it works, I do not know, but he likened it to opening ourselves to what we in Judaism call Ruach, the breath of God—or what you would call the Holy Spirit. The process is as much metaphysical as it is scientific—far beyond our understanding."

Elli looked at Cassandra as if to seek permission. Cassandra glanced at Ariella, who nodded. He then took out the necklace and held it out for Ariella to take.

"I wish this burden fell on me, young lady, and not you," he said.

"Mr. Hassan," said Luke. "Can this power allow the wearer to control life and death?"

"Unfortunately, not, my friend," said Elli. "Believe me, I asked."

Ariella looked up at Luke with sadness, clearly understanding his desperate hope to somehow see his wife and daughter again.

Luke forced a smile to reassure her and then she turned to accept the necklace from Elli. As she held it up above her head, he noticed that the smooth, flat sapphire stone in the amulet had symbols carved into it. The design looked like two interlocking circles. Within each circle was an outline of two shapes—a smaller circle and a crescent. At the center of the intersection of the two larger spheres was a marking that looked like the sun.

"What are those symbols?" he said.

"It's to symbolize the unity between our planets," said Elli. "The star in the center represents the wearer of the An'za talisman. The one who will unite us in defiance against the enemy. But be aware, Ariella cannot do this alone. She must be protected until the properties of the An'za fully assimilate into her being. I can only do so much in your country. But I will help where I can."

Luke watched as Ariella carefully put on the necklace. He wasn't sure what to expect. Time seemed to move in slow motion as the amulet rested delicately on her chest. He studied her young, innocent face. She didn't look any different. He wondered if the talisman was even working or if its alleged magic powers were just a faint, desperate hope of the dying race her father belonged to. Then he saw something. At least, he thought he did. A faint, blueish glow seemed to be reflecting off the stone and onto Ariella's face. Then, as quickly as it came, it dissipated. It might have been his imagination—or perhaps it was an illusion caused by the sun shining through the stained-glass windows.

He observed intently as Ariella placed her small, dainty hands on the necklace and felt the sapphire stone. He figured she, too, was wondering if the talisman had any effect. Then she looked toward the ceiling and said quietly, "Now, I understand, father."

♦

"What is it?" said Luke, looking at Ariella. "What do you understand?"

"Luke," she said, looking at him casually, "you were always part of this. You need to keep us hidden and get us to Death Valley."

"And then what?" said Luke.

"I'm not exactly sure, but I think I can help stop them," she said. "I *have* to try. It's why I'm here."

"Is Gideon still alive?" said Cassandra.

"I don't know," she said.

"But you communicated with him."

"His spirit spoke to me through the An'za. It's hard to explain."

"What do you feel?" said Luke.

"I feel… everything." She lifted her hand, palm-side up, and Luke could've sworn he saw a glow emanating from it.

Luke and Cassandra shot a puzzled look toward one another.

"Luke," said Ariella, putting her arms back down, "what do we do now?"

Luke pointed to himself in confusion. He was expecting her to tell *him* what to do. Now it appeared it would be up to him to get creative.

"Well, for one," he said, "we'll need to gather supplies. We'll need cash. I have a cabin in the Poconos we can use as a base. It's best to travel at night. I'll need to draw up an EPA."

"An EPA?" said his father.

"Evasion Plan of Action." He looked toward Cassandra. "Listen, we can meet tonight at George's Diner. George knows my family and he can keep a secret."

"Yes, that's perfect," said his father. "His family's been in our congregation for years."

"Let's say eight o'clock. Meanwhile, I'll prepare a plan and get whatever supplies we'll need. Cass, maybe you can pack a carry-on bag for you and Ariella with a change of clothes and toiletries, nothing larger. Do you have duct tape and a hand mirror or two?"

"I do," she said.

"Good. Bring them. As many mirrors as you can bring. We may need them for signaling. And some bobby pins and cotton pads—any kind will do."

"What are the bobby pins for?" said his father.

"I can think of about five different uses, including getting out of handcuffs. Six if you include putting your hair up in the desert. Everybody clear?"

Cassandra nodded and put her arm around Ariella.

"I'll get the word to Kevin and Brody," said his father. "And for Pete's sake, give me a shopping list. It's the least I can do if I won't be joining you."

"Fair enough, Dad," said Luke.

Luke glanced over at Elli Hassan. "Will you be joining us?"

Elli shook his head. "I'm afraid my job here is done. Rest assured, I'll be keeping a close eye on the events, and you can count on me and my compatriots doing what we can... within reason." He looked at Cassandra and smiled. "It seems your daughter is in good hands."

"Thank you," she said. "For everything."

He nodded and turned to leave, but then stopped and faced Cassandra again.

"Oh, and don't be too hard on Kersius," he said. "He was the greatest man I ever knew."

CHAPTER 14

PLAN OF ACTION

Luke was back in his house after a busy afternoon gathering supplies. He reviewed the plan he'd written up. It would take thirty-nine hours of driving time to get to Death Valley from the cabin in Lake Harmony, avoiding tolls as much as possible. Figuring thirteen hours of driving per night, they would get there in three days, which would be just in time. Driving mostly in the evening would bring the lightest traffic and the best chance of not being spotted.

Kathleen's parents had owned the Poconos cabin since she was a child. Her mother never cared for it; she was more of a beach person. But Kathleen's father used to go there during hunting season with his friends, at least before he ended up in a wheelchair and on oxygen. Since then, it's remained vacant and unused, so when Luke had called after meeting with Wilcox, her mother was all too happy to let Luke use it for whatever he needed.

Luke studied his United States map, carefully laid out on the coffee table. The route, mostly on I-80 West, would take them through nine states, including Pennsylvania; Indiana; Illinois; Iowa; Nebraska; Colorado; Utah; Nevada; and, finally,

California. He was careful to observe the rules of the standard SEAL evasion plan: Never write on the map; don't soil the map by touching the destination points; and don't fold the map in a manner that gives away your route. Of course, in this case, it wouldn't be hard to guess where they were headed. It seemed like half the country would be headed there. Still, the habit was engrained into his head, and it couldn't hurt to be too careful.

He made a mental note of exits, alternate routes, and stopping points. If hundreds of thousands of people were indeed expected to make the pilgrimage to Death Valley, he didn't want to risk getting held up by a delay. He'd already loaded his homemade SEAL kit into the car—the official one had to stay on the base—as well as other supplies, including the burner phones. Once they'd arrived at Death Valley, there wouldn't be any cell phone reception, but they'd need them en route. He'd also packed six two-liter jugs of water and four jugs filled with gasoline just in case. And, of course, his personal weapons—two hunting rifles and a 357 Magnum. He wished he had his Navy-issued rifles, but he had to turn them in after the last deployment at the UN, as per regulation.

The most difficult part of the plan would be getting everyone together to the cabin without being noticed, but he had a strategy for that as well. He'd share it with them at the diner. He checked his watch. It was seven-thirty—time to leave. As he carefully folded the map and prepared to leave the house, he heard the front door open. He turned around to see his father walking in, carrying two large bags filled with groceries.

"Glad I caught you, Luke," said his father. "Figured you could use these. All packed and non-perishable."

Luke smiled and grabbed the bags from him. "Thanks. You would've made a good SEAL."

"I'll fight in other ways, thank you. Now you be safe out

there. Let the little girl handle anything tough."

Luke laughed as he brought the bags out to the car. "Now that's a statement for the ages."

"I wish I was kidding," said his father, following him after closing the front door.

Luke loaded the bags into the car and turned to hug his father.

"Don't worry about me, Dad. I'm trained for this stuff."

"Nobody is trained for this stuff," said his father holding him and patting his back. "You just be safe."

"I will, Dad. You, too. And thanks for getting the word out to Kevin and Brody."

His father nodded.

Luke climbed into the driver side and pulled out of the driveway as his father stood watching him pull away. As he made his way to the diner to meet up with everyone, he checked the rear-view mirror periodically to make sure he wasn't being followed. So far, so good. He couldn't help but think of the old joke about the optimistic man who fell from the top floor of a building, and every floor on the way down he could be heard saying, "So far, so good."

Trying not to think about the possible horrors that awaited, Luke turned on the radio. The Rolling Stones song came on, *Sympathy for the Devil.*

◆

Before long, Luke was pulling into the parking lot at George's Diner. It was one of his favorite places growing up. Old George had since retired, but young George, who was about sixty, now ran the place. Luke knew him well as he was an active congregant in the church. Luke used to call him Saint George because he regularly donated a substantial amount of food to the poor. Fortunately, the lot wasn't overly crowded this time of night.

After parking his car, he retrieved the burner phones from his trunk and dropped them into his leather satchel. Then he headed toward the front door of the diner. Before entering, he took one last glance around the parking lot. Nothing appeared out of the ordinary.

As he walked in, he headed past the booths toward the right to a separate room designated for groups, which he'd requested from George. As soon as he entered the room, he saw Ariella and Cassandra sitting at a large table meant for twelve people, though they would only be five. Sitting across from them with their backs to Luke were Kevin Royster and Lieutenant Brody, who was in plain clothes wearing an Eagles shirt. Ariella spotted Luke immediately and waved. The only other table in the room had a large Asian family celebrating a child's birthday, at least judging by the balloons.

Luke sat next to Ariella and greeted everyone at the table, making sure to thank Royster and Brody for being there. He picked up a menu and was about to speak when he was interrupted by Ariella grabbing his arm.

"Just so you know," she said quietly to him, "there are two government agents sitting in the booth by the main entrance and there are three more outside sitting in their cars in the parking lot."

"And you know this how?" said Luke.

"I just do," she said. "Trust me."

Just then, the door to the room pushed open and the server appeared, a silver-haired woman who looked like she'd been out in the sun one too many times.

Luke's mind was running a mile a minute as the waitress took their orders. The kids at the table behind them began screaming about something, so he had to repeat his order three times. Then, finally, their mother quieted them down enough for him to be able to think straight.

"We'll have to come up with a plan to get out of here," said Luke, after the waitress left.

"I already have one," said Ariella. "Let me try."

Royster and Brody looked at one another.

"Well, I trust her," said Brody, shrugging his shoulders.

"Okay," said Luke. "So, I guess while we're waiting, I'll share the initial steps of our journey."

"The initial steps?" said Royster.

Luke handed out the burner phones, preloaded with all their phone numbers, and explained that they'd each be taking different cars and slightly alternate routes to the cabin, though all would lead to I-476 north and PA-940. Luke would be meeting his mother-in-law at the Plymouth Meeting Mall parking lot. He'd borrow her car and leave his in the lot. She'd kindly agreed to take a rideshare home. Ordinarily, he would've had the others take the bus or the train to be safe, but time was of the essence. He went over all the routes with the group.

"That's all fine and dandy," said Brody, "but how are we gonna get past those CIA agents out there in the first place. They're not gonna just let us waltz out without tracking us."

Luke glanced at Ariella.

"I already said I have a plan," said Ariella. "Besides, they're already tracking us," said Ariella. "They put trackers on all the cars while we've been sitting here."

"Dammit, is there anything you don't know?" said Brody.

"Nice shirt, Lieutenant," said Ariella, looking at his Eagles Superbowl shirt. "If it makes you feel better, I don't know when the Eagles will win the Superbowl again."

"Yeah, that's really funny," he said. "Now what exactly is your 'plan'?" He formed quotation signs with his hands. "And, by the way, I'd appreciate it if nobody calls me Lieutenant. I'm tryin' to keep a low profile."

"So, what do we call you?" said Luke.

Just then, a loud pop from behind startled him. He turned around to see one of the balloons at the other table had popped.

"Carl," said Brody. "My name's Carl."

The door pushed open again and the server arrived with their meals. Luke had ordered his usual Eggs Benedict and everyone else had burgers of one sort or another. After handing out the platters as if she were dealing cards, the server was gone in a flash, zipping off to some other table.

"To answer your question, Carl," said Ariella, "I'll be using the trackers they planted to feed them false information. They'll be miles behind us going in the wrong direction."

"You can do that!?" said Luke.

"I think I can."

"You think?" said Brody.

"But we still have to get past them," said Royster.

Ariella looked at her mother.

"Mom?" she said. "It's time."

Cassandra reached into her purse and handed out small earplugs to everyone.

"Before we leave here," said Ariella, "put these on."

"What are you going to do?" said Luke.

"Trust me, Luke. It's the best option we have."

He knew better than to question Ariella by now, so he simply nodded and then redirected his attention to his meal. Even Brody didn't say anything.

Once they finished their meals and paid the bill, Ariella instructed them to put the earplugs in and walk to their respective cars without reacting to any agents who may try to interfere.

As soon as Luke began walking past the booths, he spotted two men in the last booth on the left who were clearly agents. They were dressed in plain clothes, but he knew trained men when he saw them. There was a certain look in their eye. He didn't know how he missed them the first time. As he passed their booth, they both got up. Then something strange happened.

Both men held their ears and winced as they bent over in pain. As Luke glanced around, everyone in the diner was holding their ears. He kept walking as casually as he could until he was outside. As he strode toward his car, he spotted Ariella staring intently at two cars in the parking lot. He could see the driver of one of the cars holding his head. He couldn't see the other driver. The windows of their cars, as well as a couple cars next to them, appeared to shatter. He climbed into his car and took off, taking off the earplugs as he pulled quickly onto the road, his heart pounding.

"Well, that'll be on the news," he said to himself. He had a sinking feeling in the pit of his stomach that the war had just begun. The CIA would be on a mad hunt for them now. Fortunately, the agents would be following a bogus trail. But if he or any of his posse were spotted, all bets would be off.

CHAPTER 15

ROAD TROUBLE

Luke's mother-in-law had been waiting for him in the mall parking lot as planned. Rather than have her take the bus home, he'd decided to drop her off at her house. It wasn't that far from the mall, and besides, it had given him another chance to ensure he wasn't being followed. At one point, en route to her house, he'd thought a car was tailing him, especially since it had followed him across several turns and lane switches. Fortunately, it had turned out to be a false alarm. He'd used one of the many tricks he'd learned for confirming whether someone was following him. A red light had turned green, and instead of moving, he'd stayed put. As expected, all the cars behind him had started honking. The driver he'd thought was tailing him then hurriedly pulled around him, zipping ahead to catch the green light. That was the only close call he'd had so far, but the journey hadn't begun yet.

Now that he dropped off his mother-in-law, Luke was finally on Route 476 headed toward the Poconos. Still wary, he maintained situational awareness at all times, intentionally shifting lanes a few times and observing the actions of other cars. He'd already received a call from Cassandra informing him that she and Ariella were safely on their way. He hoped the tracking devices Ariella had rigged were leading the agents in the wrong direction as planned, but he had no reason to doubt her abilities.

He took a breath and turned on the radio to listen to the news. He was curious if there was any report about the incident at the diner, not to mention an update on the coming event in Death Valley. As soon as he flipped the station, a report was already in progress.

"As of now," said the female broadcaster, "it remains a mystery as to what caused the sonic disturbance, but some speculate it was a microwave weapon attack similar to those allegedly used against US Embassy staff in Germany in 2021 and five years earlier in Cuba and China. The question remains: Who was the attack intended for? In other news…"

Luke flipped channels again and happened upon another news update.

"As state governments prepare for the *happening*," said a male voice on the radio, "it is expected that well upwards of a hundred million people will be attending and possibly twice that. For comparison, the only public gathering in history to even approach that size was in 2019, when 120 million strong assembled for the Kumbh Mela. It was the largest ever crowd for the Hindu pilgrimage that occurs every twelve years, and, to date, is considered the largest public gathering in human history."

A commercial for an allergy drug came on, so Luke switched to a music station, Don McLean's melancholic ode to Van Gogh, "Vincent," was playing. As the words painted a delicate picture of a starry, starry night and shadows on the hills, Luke's eyes couldn't help but drift toward the evening skies on the horizon. What kind of dangers would this destructive entity be bringing from above? With a name like

Valdok the Destroyer, Luke wondered how Ariella—even a super-charged Ariella—would fare against such a universally feared power. It would seem all the armies and weapons in the world wouldn't stand a chance, which is perhaps why the government was cooperating. He wondered if they even knew who or what they were dealing with.

Indeed, he felt small and weak compared to threats of such magnitude, and yet Ariella said he had a crucial role to play. He thought about it. Theologically, if Ariella represented Moses, or more accurately Moses and Aaron combined—deliverer and prophet—perhaps his role was more like Joshua, the humble servant and warrior—the chosen assistant. It was a role he was more than happy to play. He only hoped it would make a difference.

His mind wandered to the upcoming event. He tried to imagine what a crowd of a couple hundred million people would even look like. He remembered seeing footage of the massive throngs at Woodstock, and that was only half a million people. This could be several hundred times that. In a place like Death Valley, where the temperatures routinely soared above a hundred degrees, it sounded like a humanitarian crisis waiting to happen. And where in Death Valley would this 'happening' even be held? From what he'd read, Death Valley was over a hundred and forty miles long and about ten miles wide. The only thing the news reports said was that signage would direct visitors and that updates would be forthcoming, so clearly the government was in the know. Of course, to what degree they were involved or informed remained to be seen, or whether they even knew this was an alien threat.

He thought back to Ariella and Cassandra and wondered what new revelations Ariella might be sharing at the moment. She seemed well tuned in. He'd already made up his mind that when, and if, all this was behind them, he'd like to see more of them both. But first, they'd need to survive. And for the first time in his life, he questioned if there'd even be a world to survive in.

◆

"You know he likes you," said Ariella, licking a double-scoop chocolate ice cream cone with rainbow sprinkles.

"You're spilling half of that on my car seat," said Cassandra, trying to keep her eyes on the road as she drove.

"You were the one who decided to get ice cream."

"Fair enough." In the great scheme of things, the stupid car seat probably didn't even matter anymore.

"Anyway, I mean he really likes you. I think you two should get together."

"Ariella! Don't pry."

"I'm just saying."

"Well, that's enough saying."

"Ow!"

Cassandra turned to see Ariella holding her head as if she were in pain. Her sapphire blue An'za amulet was glowing.

"What's wrong!?"

Ariella was wincing and starting to yell out.

"Ariella! Should I pull over?"

"Keep driving!" said Ariella, frantically, as her face turned to one of deep concentration. She was still holding her head.

"What's happening? Talk to me." The amulet was still glowing.

"They're tracking me. I think they've always been tracking me. I'm trying to stop it. I... I'm listening to them. I hear them."

"Hear who?"

"There's giant sand dunes up ahead. They're singing."

"Who's singing?"

"I hear voices coming from the sand. Deep voices, like a giant choir. And bodies everywhere. Dead bodies. Wait… I'm in his head now."

"Whose head? Ariella, whose head are you in?"

"Valdok."

Cassandra looked at her daughter who was staring straight ahead as if in a trance.

"Ariella, what's happening?"

Her daughter didn't answer.

"Talk to me. What's happening."

"Aaagh!" Ariella put her hands on her head again as she cried out in pain. "It burns! It burns!"

Frantic, Cassandra cut across two lanes to the right to pull over to the side of the road. All she could do was listen helplessly to her daughter's anguish, as the driver behind them blasted his horn. Just as her car skidded safely onto the shoulder of the highway, the screaming stopped.

Cassandra glanced over at Ariella, whose face had now turned from pain and fear to one of steadfast determination. The brave young girl was grasping her amulet in her hand.

"Get out, Valdok," said Ariella, sneering. Then she took a deep breath as the amulet returned to its normal shade of sapphire blue.

"Ariella, are you okay? Tell me what happened."

"Valdok… He was tracking me. I think it stopped for now, but I'm not sure for how long. He's strong. A lot stronger than me."

"What about the sand? You said something about sand dunes and singing."

"It was one of my visions. I think it was the future. But that's not the biggest problem right now. I used Valdok's connection to get into his head before he shut me out."

"What did you see? What's going to happen to all those people in Death Valley?"

"It's much worse than that," said Ariella. "It's bad. We have to warn Luke."

Cassandra's hands shook as she fumbled with the phone in her purse. When she finally got it out and tried to use it, all she saw was a black screen. It should've had a full battery. She fished for the charger in the glove compartment.

"Don't bother," said Ariella. "It won't work. Valdok fried it."

Cassandra's heart skipped a beat. "He can do that?"

"He can do a lot of things," said Ariella. "Even more than I can. And he knew where we were, so I suggest we get moving."

CHAPTER 16

CABIN PRESSURE

After driving on Route 903 North for about an hour, Luke made a left onto Lake Harmony Road. Lake Harmony was one of the most beautiful reservoirs in the Pocono Mountains, punctuated by majestic waterfalls and scenic nature trails and a stone's throw from the Jack Frost and Big Boulder ski resorts. Any other time, he'd be thrilled to enjoy its beckoning outdoor adventures. He regretted not coming here with Kathleen and Kayla, but something else always seemed to come up, not the least of which was his time overseas.

As he passed the Kidder Township Police Department on the right, he remained on alert. For all he knew, every police department in the country had his photo by now, but at night he wouldn't have been easily spotted unless he were stopped for some reason. He followed the road around to the left until it turned into South Lake Drive. Then he scanned the addresses opposite the banks of Lake Harmony until he spotted the cabin. Even in the dark, he could recognize the two-story stone structure with the two bright red rocking chairs on the porch and the huge wooden deck overlooking the lake. It looked just like the pictures.

As planned, he was the first one to arrive. He pulled onto the gravel driveway beside the cabin and parked. Before leaving the car, he called Brody and Royster to let them know it was clear to approach. They were both about a half hour away. He tried calling Cassandra several times, but it kept going to her voice mail. He left a message and hoped she'd see it.

Relieved that all seemed quiet, but slightly concerned about Cassandra and Ariella, he left the car and approached the cabin. It was dark around the perimeter, but from the window it seemed a light was on inside the cabin. He peered into the window but didn't see anyone. It was possible Kathleen's mother kept the lights on a timer for safety, though she hadn't mentioned it, and she was usually pretty specific about every little detail under the sun, from how to turn on the water valves to which detergent to use for the laundry.

Just to be careful, he opened his trunk and took out his 357 Magnum. He made his way to the front door and tried the knob. It wasn't locked. It dawned on him he might be walking into an ambush. He kicked the door open slowly and immediately backed up against the outside wall with his gun ready.

"You can come out," he shouted. "I know you're in there. Do it slowly. I'm armed."

"At ease, Petty Officer Remington," said a loud voice from inside. It was Admiral Hargrove.

"What are you doing here, Admiral?"

"A house call. You and I have some catching up to do. You may as well come in."

Luke wasn't sure what was going on. How did Hargrove know he'd be here? He wondered whether to warn the others and tell them not to come.

"It's okay, Remington," said Hargrove. The admiral took a

more casual, friendly tone, no doubt sensing his hesitation. "Wilcox sent me. How the hell else would I know to come here? Think about it."

Luke let out a deep breath, put the gun at his side, and entered the cabin. Hargrove was standing in the living room, along with Captain Martinez. Luke saluted them both and they saluted back.

"Admiral, I—"

"Remington, nothing about this visit is official. But I think we both know that there's something going on that's above all of us, and I mean that literally and figuratively. I know about the girl, at least what Wilcox told me. Her file's protected and they're calling her the *asset*, but Wilcox thinks they mean something else and so do I. Now Wilcox didn't tell me everything. He said I should hear it from you and that's why we're here."

Luke took a seat on one of the large, cushion armchairs.

"You may need to sit down, too," he said.

He watched as Hargrove and Martinez took a seat on the long, hunter green couch opposite him.

"Ariella isn't what you may think," said Luke. "She and this Jesus imposter have more power than you can possibly imagine. Except she's trying to help us, and she just may be our only hope."

"Luke," said Martinez, "you forget I was at the UN, too. I saw what he did. He was like a god."

"He practically *is* a god. Just not the one people think. He's from a planet about six thousand light years away, and it seems he has an especially nasty reputation of killing other worlds by posing as deities. Now I guess it's our turn."

"How on the real God's green earth would you know that?" said Hargrove, who remained as stone-faced as always, but was no doubt skeptical.

"It's a long story."

"Well, we have time."

"Not as much as I'd like," said Luke.

Luke explained what he'd witnessed at the church, the message from Kersius, Ariella's purpose, and his role in it. Hargrove and Martinez kept looking at each other in disbelief.

"So, you're saying this Valdok character is like a planet killer," said Martinez, leaning forward. "And this girl's alien father impregnated a human to give birth to a hybrid child who's supposed to save our planet with the help of a magic necklace."

"The An'za," said Luke.

"I think I need a drink."

"I wish I could tell you I'm making all this up," said Luke, "but I'm not."

"A few weeks ago, I would've thought you were on drugs," said Martinez. "But now? You could tell me a hundred-foot-tall talking Chihuahua is gonna save the planet and I'd buy it."

"If all this alien mumbo jumbo is true," said Hargrove, "then the government's just leading the pigs to slaughter."

"It sure sounds like it," said Luke. "They're probably being sacrificed so he'll leave the rest of the planet alone. The only hope we have is to get Ariella to Death Valley and hope she can make a difference before all those people disappear."

"Can't we warn them?" said Martinez.

Hargrove shook his head. "Officially, we can't do anything. We'd be silenced and branded as idiots. Unofficially, all we can do is make sure that girl gets to Death Valley. But the bigger question is whether we want to do anything at all."

"I'm not following," said Luke.

"It's simple. What if everything went right? Let's say against all odds, we managed to save all those people and prevent them from marching to their deaths. The enemy is called Valdok the Destroyer, not Valdok the Bargainer. His reaction is just as likely to be to attack the whole planet if his sacrificial lambs are taken away."

"That's why we have Ariella," said Luke. "So, he doesn't get that chance."

"That's quite a lot you're betting on that little girl," said Hargrove. "All I'm saying is, by trying to interfere, we could be putting the whole planet in danger."

Before Luke could even process the dilemma, Luke heard a car pull up onto the gravel driveway outside.

"Is that her?" said Hargrove.

"I hope," said Luke. He went outside as Hargrove and Martinez waited.

As soon as Luke stepped outside, he saw Brody parking in his blue Nissan. Kevin Royster pulled in just behind him. Still no sign of Cassandra with Ariella. Luke tried calling them again but couldn't get through.

♦

Luke greeted Brody and Royster and told them about Hargrove and Martinez. He ushered them in the front door.

"Admiral, this is Lieutenant Carl Brody with the Philadelphia Police and my old friend, Marine Sergeant Kevin Royster who I met in Afghanistan when I was a chaplain. They're part of our little crew and are risking their necks to be here."

"Join the club," said Martinez, as he and Hargrove stood.

"Welcome to crazytown, gentlemen," said Hargrove.

Royster saluted him and Hargrove saluted back.

"Those are some bad burns, Sergeant," said Hargrove.

"Got it in Kabul when my Jeep ran over an IED," said Royster. "I wouldn't be here today if Luke hadn't risked his life to save me."

"You would've done the same for me," said Luke.

"Well, that's what Remington... er Luke... does," said

Hargrove. He turned to Luke. "You don't mind if I call you Luke, now that we're all in this great big mess together."

"Not at all, uh.. what do I call you?"

"Call me Admiral." He redirected his attention to Royster. "Anyway, Luke and I were just discussing a little dilemma we have."

"You mean the traffic?" said Brody. "I just heard on the radio they're shuttin' down a bunch of airports. They started with Harry Reid in Nevada. No flights in or out. That means the roads'll be a mess. The hell with dyin' in Death Valley. They'll probably die on the way there."

"And how about all those people putting up roadblocks everywhere?" said Royster. "That's just gonna make it worse."

"I'm afraid I'm talking about a different dilemma," said Hargrove. "If we manage to stop this event in Death Valley— and that's a very big *if*—we may be taking candy away from a tremendously big baby. And his tantrum just might put the rest of the world in danger."

"The rest of the world is already in danger," said a young girl's voice from the front door.

"It's Ariella!" said Luke, as she and Cassandra came in. He looked at them in bewilderment. "How come we didn't hear you pull up?"

"Because I didn't want you to," said Ariella. "There were strangers here."

"Ah yes," said Luke, "Ariella, I'd like you to meet Admiral Hargrove and Captain Martinez. They're on our side."

She looked at them both for an awkward moment.

"So they are," she said. "I can sense it. But your theories are all wrong."

"How so?" said Hargrove, looking perplexed.

"Valdok tried to track me on the way here. I was able to hold him off for now, but he's strong. He'll find us again, and soon. But I managed to access his thoughts for a few seconds.

Enough to know their plan."

"You did!?" said Luke. "What is it?"

"It's bad, Luke. Certain members of the United States government are under the belief that if they allow people to go to Death Valley to be taken by Valdok, he'll leave the rest of the planet alone. That was the deal they made."

Hargrove elbowed Luke. "What did I tell you?" he said.

"Valdok doesn't make deals," said Ariella. "The people who'll be taken in Death Valley, like all the people he's taken so far, will be used as slaves until they die."

"Slaves for what?" said Luke.

"To mine for resources after the end."

"The end of what?" said Hargrove.

"Everything on Earth."

"What!?" said Hargrove.

"His plan is to use the taken ones as slaves and destroy the rest of humanity. That's what he does with every planet. It's what he did to my father's planet."

Luke didn't know what to think. He was still trying to process it.

"Does this change our plan?" he said. "How do we even stop something like that?"

"Our plans don't change," said Ariella. "We have to try to stop him in Death Valley. It's our only hope. And I'll need you there too, Luke. I'll need all of you. And there's something else. I saw a vision. Giant sand dunes. And they were singing, like a deep chorus.

"Eureka!" said Martinez, standing at the back of the group.

"What did you find?" said Hargrove.

"No, I mean the singing sands. It's at the Eureka Sand Dunes in Death Valley. They have enormous dunes, and they make a sound like they're singing. That's where it'll take place."

"It has to be that," said Luke. "And the more they delay announcing it, the bigger advantage we'll have getting there sooner than the masses."

"So, the early bird gets the alien god," said Brody. "Not sure I like the sound of that."

"There's more," said Ariella. "In my vision, there was fighting, a lot of fighting. With weapons like nothing you've ever seen."

"What kind of weapons?" said Martinez.

Ariella looked at him unemotionally. "Imagine a legion from ancient Rome fighting against the full power of your greatest technology today. That's the odds we're dealing with."

Luke knew it wasn't his imagination that her vocabulary sounded like it had aged ten years since he'd seen her last.

"We're just a small group," said Martinez. "We don't have anything that could combat that kind of threat."

"You have me," she said.

"You!? I know you have special abilities and all that, but—"

"Captain," said Cassandra, directing her attention to Martinez, "I watched my daughter fend off some kind of mind attack from Valdok himself and read his thoughts. If her father says she can help us against this threat, then I believe him."

"That's all fine and good," said Martinez, "but we only have the tech we brought with us, which isn't a lot."

"When the time comes," said Ariella, "I will do whatever I can. It may not be enough, but it'll be better than whatever technology you would've brought."

"How?" said Martinez.

"I can feel it. I'm getting stronger."

"You can feel it? That's supposed to make me feel better?"

"Guys," said Royster, speaking up for the first time, "think about it. What choice do we have?"

"Agreed," said Hargrove. "So, it seems our trip to Death Valley is on."

Martinez nodded. "When do we head out, sir?"

"Now. We can't afford to wait for morning. And the fewer cars we take, the better. We can take turns sleeping."

Luke looked over at Cassandra and Ariella. "I'll go with the two of you," he said.

"No," said Ariella. "We need to go separately. My mother and I will go with Admiral Hargrove and Captain Martinez. And—"

"Wait," said Martinez. "How did you know our names?"

Ariella glanced at him, then looked back at Luke and smirked.

"Anyway," she said to Luke, "you and I need to be in separate cars in case they come after me. I've already put you in too much danger, and I need you at Death Valley alive."

Luke directed his attention to Brody and Royster. "So, it looks like the three of us will go together," he said.

"Fine by me," said Brody. "More of us to take turns driving."

Luke contemplated what would no doubt be a harrowing journey ahead. These were unprecedented times. There was no way to really prepare for something like this.

He caught up to Kevin Royster as they headed out the door of the cabin and put his arm on his shoulder.

"Well," he said, "once more into the breach, dear friend. Once more into the breach."

CHAPTER 17

INTO THE SPIDER'S WEB

L ance Kilgore didn't fear much, but when he was standing face to face with a superior being who clearly wasn't happy, he couldn't help but feel his palms begin to sweat. As if he needed a reminder who he was dealing with, he glanced out the window of the spacecraft into the vastness of space and contemplated how to tell his celestial host the bad news. Fortunately, this time he had the president with him. He decided to be straightforward.

"I haven't located the girl yet," he said. "We're not exactly dealing with a normal human here."

"You are not dealing with a human at all," said Valdok, who had once again taken on the appearance of an older man, though still an imposing one. "She is more Alaktian than human, and yet... something more. Curious. Nevertheless, I have located her."

Though baffled by Valdok's revelation, Kilgore breathed a sigh of relief. "Where is she? I'll go immediately."

"You will not," said Valdok. "You are no match for her. I have other plans for you. And I will deal with her in my own way."

"Your own way?" said Kilgore. "What exactly is an Alaktian, anyway?"

"A far superior race than yours that I dealt with expediently. Except for whatever remains in her, they no longer exist."

"This cannot escalate," said the president, turning to face them. He'd been standing looking out into the cosmos. "Only the Chair of the Joint Chiefs and Special Agent Kilgore's unit know anything about this arrangement of ours, and I'd like to keep it that way. Even my Chief of Staff and the Vice President remain blissfully unaware. Hell, I haven't even told the First Lady."

"The girl *is* aware," said Valdok, "and so are her comrades. Even now, she is arranging to split their forces, to which, I might add, she has added two men from your navy."

The president's eyes widened.

"Who are they?" said Kilgore.

"It is unimportant. As the spider lures the fly, I am leading them into a trap."

"Don't be so sure," said Kilgore. "That girl is scary smart."

"Not as smart as she believes. I even let her into my head briefly, for good reason. I remain one step ahead of her at every turn."

"I hope so," said the president. "Because if this blows up, I won't be able to honor our deal."

"Let me remind you," said Valdok, "that our *deal* is to grant your kind the precious opportunity to live while we accept your sacrificial offering. As a gesture of goodwill, we will provide you the technology you asked. Should you decide not to honor our generosity, or should we not receive the resources we were promised, all bets—as your kind likes to say—are off, and you shall go the way of the Alaktians. Do I make myself clear?"

Kilgore watched as the president contemplated the

ultimatum, a wasteful gesture as it was crystal clear who held all the cards in this particular conversation.

"You do," said the president.

"Delighted," said Valdok, sneering.

"You said you have other plans for me," said Kilgore. "What exactly do they entail?"

Valdok smiled. "If I am the spider," he said, "then you will represent the web."

"I don't understand."

"I will explain. Come with me."

Valdok looked at the president. "Wait here."

Kilgore followed his otherworldly host down a brightly lit corridor while the president did as he was told.

The alien managed to be just as intimidating in human form—a dominating presence clearly accustomed to being obeyed. He couldn't imagine what kind of task was in store for him.

◆

Cassandra had been driving for five hours on I-80 West and was getting exhausted. They were approaching Akron, Ohio. Ariella had fallen asleep in the back seat next to Martinez, and Hargrove was napping in the front passenger seat. Brody had given her his burner phone, as he said he wouldn't need it driving with Luke. She'd used it once so far to call Luke when she'd lost sight of his car for a half hour. Fortunately, he'd been staying within view most of the way.

It was nearing two in the morning and her eyes were starting to play tricks on her—the taillights from trucks in the distance would occasionally blend with the road reflectors and highway signs. On a few occasions, the lanes ahead of her appeared to cross. She knew it was probably time to ask Hargrove to take a turn driving, but she figured she'd stretch it out another hour.

As Cassandra drove, she felt the car slowing down. She glanced at the fuel indicator, and she still had half a tank left. She pressed the gas pedal, but the car wouldn't go above fifty miles an hour. She watched as Luke's car passed them. No doubt they were wondering why she was slowing down. She checked to make sure her cruise control wasn't on, and it wasn't. Besides, pressing the gas pedal would've overridden it.

"Dammit!" she whispered, so as not to wake everyone. This was the worst possible time for the car to be acting up. Just then, she saw police lights up ahead. They seemed to be following Luke's car.

"Admiral," she said, nudging Hargrove. "We have a problem."

Hargrove jolted awake and was immediately alert upon seeing the police lights up ahead. "Get in the left lane and keep going," he said. "We'll worry about Remington after. And why oh why are we going so slow? It'll draw attention."

"I don't have a choice," she said. "The car won't go above fifty."

"What!?" he said.

The car began to pull to the right.

"Well, don't pull over!" said Hargrove.

"I'm not doing it!" Cassandra was starting to panic now. The car slowed down and began spinning out of control toward the shoulder of the highway.

"There's something wrong with the car," said Cassandra, gripping the wheel to no avail.

"It's not the car," said Ariella from the back. "They're here."

"Who's here?"

"Is this your Valdok buddy?" said Hargrove.

"It's not him," said Ariella. "It's one of his ships."

"Ships?" said Hargrove. "I don't see a damn thing."

As the car skidded to a halt on the shoulder, just shy of a ditch along the side of the road, Cassandra turned around to check on Ariella. She was tilting her head and staring up toward the roof of the car.

"Well, look at that," said Hargrove. He grabbed Cassandra's arm to redirect her attention to the front window.

A massive, oval spacecraft appeared just ahead of the car, about twice the size of a Boeing jet. It hovered in complete silence, two bands of green lights spinning around its circumference.

"It looks like one of those Tic Tac-shaped UAPs in the Navy reports," he said, "but I have to say that's one big Tic Tac. A helluva lot bigger than I would've expected."

Martinez sprung awake. "What the—"

"What's it doing?" said Hargrove. "It's just hovering."

"I don't think they want to harm us," said Ariella.

"Do *they* know that?" said Hargrove.

"If they wanted us dead, we'd be dead already," she said. "They're trying to delay us."

"Why?" said Cassandra.

"Valdok wants to meet me face to face. I can sense it. He wants us to get to Death Valley. Just not yet. And not all of us."

"What do you mean not all of us?" said Martinez.

Just then, the enormous craft shot up in the sky like a bullet, silently disappearing in an instant.

"Unbelievable!" said Hargrove. "That defied every possible law of physics!"

"Luke and the others were taken," said Ariella, matter-of-factly. "This was just a decoy."

"Taken by *them*?" said Cassandra, pointing to the sky.

"No, not them. The CIA has them. Kilgore. That's what those police lights were all about."

"That's mighty bad for them, but *we* have to keep going,"

said Hargrove. "We can't give up now. Besides, they'll have been taken to a secure safehouse. Needle in a haystack and all that. And we don't have time to look though haystacks."

"We can't go without Luke!" shouted Ariella.

"But we have to, honey," said Cassandra. "Luke would want us to."

"You don't understand," said Ariella. "Luke has to be in Death Valley with us. He has to. That's why Valdok had him taken from us. We have to get him back!"

"But we don't even know where he is."

"And he'll be well guarded, believe me," said Hargrove.

Ariella took a breath and then the otherworldly look of steadfast confidence that Cassandra knew all too well returned to her face.

"I know where he is," she said. "We have to get him."

"Well, we can't just go waltzing in there, wherever *there* is," said Hargrove.

"They're being taken to the Wright-Patterson Air Force Base."

"That's three hours from here."

"They're on a plane," said Ariella.

"To Wright-Patt?"

"Near Hangar 18 to be specific."

"Hangar 18!" said Hargrove. "That doesn't even exist anymore. And even if it did, it would be locked down like Area 51. There's no way we—"

"It does exist," said Ariella. "And I'm going to lead us there."

CHAPTER 18

PRISONERS

Luke sat quietly in his chair as he glanced around the room he was thrown in with Brody and Royster. Three men, three folding chairs. Aside from that, the room was just four concrete walls, a single light hanging from the wooden ceiling, and a solid metal door. He had no clue where they were, as they'd been tied and blindfolded as soon as Kilgore and his men had taken them. One thing was for sure, this was a black site of some sort. At least they weren't tied up anymore.

"I'm surprised they put us together," said Brody.

"For now," said Luke. "They'll probably take us one at a time. Play us off one another. It's a psychological game now."

"Can't be any worse than Afghanistan," said Royster. "What do you think happened to Cassandra and Ariella?"

Luke shook his head. "Dunno. That girl can handle herself though."

"And everyone else, too," said Brody.

"Listen," said Luke. "The SEALS put us through some pretty rigorous training, to say the least. When they take you, they're gonna try and get you rattled. Don't fall for it."

"Only name, rank, and serial number, right?" said Royster. "That's what I was taught."

"I don't have a serial number," said Brody.

"Doesn't matter," said Luke. "The Geneva Conventions don't apply here. This isn't war and we're not in enemy territory."

"Coulda fooled me," said Brody.

"The key is to be the grey man," said Luke. "We learned that from the Brits. Don't be too aggressive, but don't be overly submissive either. Let them think they've got one over on you. Try to appear physically weaker than you are, like you're in pain or exhausted. But stay alert. Find a spot on the wall or the floor to focus on. Something to help you resist. Remember, they want to see how much we know and what our plans are."

"Wait a minute," said Royster. "Shouldn't we tell them what Ariella said? Maybe he doesn't know the whole world's in danger."

"It's possible, but we can't chance it yet. If they know and they were promised an escape route, we don't want to let them know we know. At least not yet. We can't put Ariella in danger."

"Why not?" said Brody. "She can handle herself. Besides, it's not like we can help anyone from here. And once that Valdok character takes over, then it's too late. You heard what she said. We have to be there with her. So everyone's toast unless we can get these guys to understand."

"I agree with Luke," said Royster. "What if they already know and they're going along with it? Maybe they were promised safety or something."

"Well, then they're even bigger morons than I think they are." Brody stood up and paced around, then stopped. "Nah, they're not stupid," he added. "They're desperate. They're desperate to make this deal with the devil. We need to make them *less* desperate."

Before Luke could think about what Brody said, a door latch made a loud noise and the thick metal door opened. Kilgore entered, flanked by two guards with assault rifles. A third man came in carrying three sacks. He tossed one to Luke and the others to Brody and Royster.

Luke opened his sack. It was a meal kit.

"Make yourself at home," said Kilgore. "You'll be here a while. Sorry, we don't have any TV in here."

"Do you always make a habit of imprisoning American citizens?" said Brody.

"Only when they threaten national security, Lieutenant."

"Seems to me we didn't break any laws."

"Consider yourself detained for your own safety."

"I kinda felt safer out there," said Brody.

Kilgore gave a half smile and turned to leave.

"So, what is it you wanna know?" said Brody. Luke wasn't sure what he was getting at.

"Know?" said Kilgore, turning around. "We already know everything we need to. You were clearly headed to Death Valley to help a certain little girl. Trust me, there's nothing you can tell me I don't already know. All I need from you is to stay here. Out of trouble."

"What kind of trouble?" said Brody. "Just what is it you think we're helping her do?"

Now Luke got it. Brody was a pretty savvy cop.

Kilgore approached. "You know as well as I what we're dealing with. This is above all of us."

"Educate me," said Brody. "What *are* we dealing with? Maybe I don't know as much as you think I do."

Kilgore peered at Brody. "How we handle this situation is classified, Lieutenant. We're not taking any chances on you or anyone else going rogue trying to solve it. Now, I think that's all I have to say on the matter."

He turned to head toward the steel doors, where his men were waiting.

"Well, we have some things to say," said Luke. "Things you'll want to hear."

Kilgore stopped and turned around again.

Luke stood and the men quickly aimed their weapons at him.

"Special Agent, you've seen firsthand what Ariella can do. But I assure you, you haven't seen all of it. She has, let's just say, some kind of psychic connection to these… beings. She knows what they're up to."

"You're not telling me anything I don't already know, Remington."

"What you *think* you know. You think by sacrificing these people in Death Valley, you're saving the rest of the world."

Kilgore's eyes looked like they were going to pop out of his head.

"I can assure you," continued Luke, "that couldn't be further from the truth. Valdok's true intention is—"

"Wait a minute. Who's Valdok?"

"That's his name. The alien entity you've been dealing with. It's only part of his name though. He's known throughout the universe as Valdok the Destroyer. Maybe you don't know as much as you think."

"Go on."

"Valdok's modus operandi is to take what he needs and obliterate the rest. Those people in Death Valley aren't there to be killed. They're there to be taken and doomed to a life of servitude and slavery—at least for as long as they're needed."

"You missed the part about saving billions," said Kilgore.

"And you missed the part about obliterating the rest. Valdok isn't here to harvest the planet. He's here to destroy it. All you're doing is helping him gain some slaves before he does it. What did he promise you? Technology? Safety? It's all a lie."

Kilgore was silent. Then he smiled. "It's a nice try. Really, it is. Very creative. Except if he's truly going to wipe everyone out as you say, why wouldn't he just do it? I'm sure he could take a few hundred thousand people first if he wanted. Just suck them up into that spaceship of his. Child's play. He wouldn't need us. So, I'm afraid you've been misinformed."

"Ariella doesn't make mistakes."

"Once again, you're wrong. She just made one. She lost the three of you. This Valdok, if that's his name, has her in his sights. He's always a step ahead of her. You know, she's the one you should be worried about. How do you know *she* isn't the villain here. She's not even human. She's an—"

"An Alaktian. I know. Half-Alaktian actually. And she has a…" Luke paused. He decided he'd shared enough. He was almost about to tell Kilgore about the necklace.

"She has a what?"

"She has… abilities that can help us."

"Or kill us all," said Kilgore. "I've seen her abilities up close. I'll take my chances with the shape-shifting alien who made us a reasonable deal. Kids creep me out."

"A reasonable deal?" said Brody, chiming in. "We're talking the end of humanity here. And you'll be the guy that helps it happen."

"You're making a deal with the devil," said Royster.

"What's that old saying?" said Kilgore. "Ah yes. The devil you know is better than the devil you don't. Have a nice night, gentleman."

He turned again to leave.

"You're making a horrible mistake, Kilgore," yelled Luke. "You need to listen to us."

"I'll take it under advisement," said Kilgore without turning around.

CHAPTER 19

A DISTURBANCE AT WRIGHT-PATTERSON

Cassandra knew the Wright-Patterson Airforce Base all too well. It was the site of Project Blue Book, the secretive government study of UFOs that was allegedly terminated in 1969—which seemed ironic given their mission. But more personal to her, it was where she did her internship in clinical psychology, at Wright-Patterson Medical Center.

Spanning 12.5 miles and boasting over 30,000 employees, the complex was vast. From shopping facilities to childcare centers, it was more like a city. Without Ariella, it would've been no small feat trying to find where Luke and the others may have been taken. Fortunately, they had Ariella, though the first trick would be getting past the entry gate without visitor passes. To get visitor passes, they would've needed to reveal their identification. That was out of the question.

"We're a mile out from the base," she said to no one in particular. "What's the plan?"

"Visitors arrive through Gate 12A," said Hargrove. "But I'm assuming we're not checking in to Visiting Quarters or this'll be over before it started."

"No, we're not," said Ariella from the back seat. Follow

the signs for Area B and the Main Gate." Cassandra had no clue how Ariella knew the layout and didn't bother to ask.

"But we can't show our ID," said Martinez.

"Don't worry about the ID," said Ariella.

Following the signs as Ariella directed, soon Cassandra could see the ticket booths up ahead that stretched across several lanes with a large, curved overhang. Each car was stopped, apparently to show their Military ID passes.

Now it was their turn.

"ID?" said the uniformed attendant.

Cassandra looked at him like a deer in the headlights when the man suddenly held his head as if he was in excruciating pain. The barrier opened on its own.

"Drive," said Ariella, matter-of-factly.

Cassandra drove through the gate.

"He's going to send someone after us," she said.

"He won't remember us," said Ariella. "Follow the signs toward NASIC."

"That's the Intelligence Center," said Cassandra. "That's where they're being kept?"

"No," said Ariella. "But it'll get us close."

They made their way past the medical center where Cassandra did her internship, then drove past the golf course on the right.

"That's it up ahead," said Ariella. "Park in the lot. We'll walk from there."

Cassandra found a spot in the parking lot in front of the modern building with horizontal, tinted glass windows and a large sign on the front that said, *National Air & Space Intelligence Center.*

"Take your backpacks," said Ariella. "You'll need them."

After they exited the car, Ariella headed to the left of the NASIC building. She seemed to know where she was going. She led them around several other buildings adjacent to the main facility. Around the back were other structures that supported the base. Behind that was a row of trees and yet more buildings, part of the enormous office complex.

Cassandra and the others followed as Ariella led them to the right through a set of trees that blocked the view of a nondescript grey building with a hangar around the back. A fence stood between them and the target destination, with a well-guarded gate. Ariella moved forward as if there wasn't a problem in the world.

As they approached the gate, two guards came running out, clearly having spotted two Navy men, a woman, and a child that didn't belong there. Ariella casually raised a hand and the men collapsed, holding their heads.

An alarm sounded. Cassandra looked to see another man in the booth by the gate. As he came running out, he, too, collapsed and joined the others. The alarm blaring, Ariella proceeded past them toward the building and Cassandra, Hargrove, and Martinez followed.

"I'm glad she's on our side," said Martinez.

Hargrove offered a nervous smile.

Ariella led them through an unmarked door. As soon as they entered the facility, six operatives dressed in black combat gear came running into the corridor and aimed their assault rifles.

"Stop there," yelled one of the men.

The alarm was still blaring.

Cassandra stopped, but Ariella slowly walked forward.

"I said stop! Lady, get control of your kid!"

"Hold your fire," shouted Hargrove over the sound of the alarm.

"On who's authority?'

Hargrove didn't answer.

Cassandra watched as Ariella kept moving forward.

"On who's authority!" yelled the man.

"Last warning," said another operative. "Stop the kid or we fire."

"Ariella, stop," said Cassandra. She knew she wouldn't stop, but thought it might buy some time.

Then Ariella stopped. The alarm was still sounding.

Cassandra observed as each of the men's guns twisted and bent toward their own faces. They looked horrified. Then, in unison, they collapsed.

Ariella raised her hand and the alarm stopped.

One of the operatives' communicators sounded and a voice came through the speaker.

"Secret Squirrel, everything okay there?"

Hargrove picked up the communicator. "All clear. It was an electrical issue. Over and out."

"Roger that," said the voice.

Just as they prepared to continue past the fallen operatives, Special Agent Kilgore appeared. He seemed shocked by what he saw.

"What did you do!?" he said, looking at Ariella.

"Where are they?" she said.

"You're wasting your time. You won't make it off the base."

"Let me worry about that," she said. She smiled. Then Kilgore collapsed.

"You do know you can't just go around leaving dead bodies," said Hargrove. "Eventually, it'll come back to bite us."

"They're sleeping," she said. "By the time they wake up, we'll be gone."

"But we still have to get out of the base."

"I'll figure it out."

"Figure it out, huh?"

She led them down the corridor to a large steel door. With a wave of her hand, the door crumbled to dust. Cassandra thought she'd seen everything from Ariella, but this was getting downright scary.

Luke, Brody, and Royster were standing there dumbfounded.

"Sorry it took so long," said Ariella. "We should go."

Cassandra embraced Luke while Hargrove helped Brody and Royster climb over the dust and rubble.

As they made their way past the fallen guards and their twisted weapons, Brody looked down, smiled, and shook his head. Then he threw up his hands as they walked.

Luke said to Brody, "What are you thinking?"

"I'm thinking Maurice Chevalier was right when he sung that damn line."

"What line's that?" said Luke.

"Thank Heaven for Little Girls."

As they exited the building, Cassandra knew something was wrong immediately. She could hear the familiar rotors up above. She knew that sound.

"Well, that's not good," said Hargrove.

She looked up to see three AH-64E Apache attack helicopters hovering overhead. Kilgore must've called them before he appeared. The corridor was no doubt being monitored.

As a gathering of armed special forces and airmen approached, a booming voice came over a speaker from one of the copters.

"Surrender immediately. This is your only warning. Discard all weapons and put your hands up."

CHAPTER 20

HANGAR 18

The whirring of the copters filled the air.

"Don't listen to them," said Ariella, over the deafening noise.

Easy for *her* to say.

Luke was happy to be rescued, but for the first time, he was beginning to wonder if Ariella really did have everything under control. She was, after all, a young girl, albeit a highly advanced one. True, she'd disabled a whole corridor full of operatives, turned their assault weapons to spaghetti, and disintegrated a steel door. But he couldn't imagine a way out of this where nobody got hurt—or killed.

"Follow me," she said, as if she were instructing a group of schoolchildren.

"Ariella, are you sure?" said Cassandra.

"This is where we need to go, Mother. Don't pay attention to them."

She walked to the left. Luke grabbed Cassandra's hand and they walked with her. Hargrove, Martinez, Brody, and Royster stood back, hesitatingly, but began to follow.

A single shot came from one of the copters. Luke jumped,

but the shot didn't seem to make contact anywhere. Then another came, and another. Ariella continued walking. He turned to see Hargrove and the others paused in confusion, glancing around as if to assess the damage, but then they continued following.

A barrage of gunfire came from the ground forces, and those shots, too, didn't seem to have any effect. It was as if Ariella had put up some sort of invisible force field protecting them.

The troops began to rush them, and Luke braced himself ready to make a run for it. Then he watched as the men stopped short, some of them bouncing back and falling on the ground. It *was* a force field. He could see the men rising again, shaken and dazed, no doubt wondering what they'd bumped into. Many more airmen stayed back, not even trying to enter the area. He thought that odd.

Then it dawned on him. They didn't have authorization. This was, after all, a top secret, secured area.

"Where is she taking us?" yelled Hargrove.

"She has a plan," shouted Luke over the noise. "*At least I hope so*," he muttered to himself."

"She said something about Hangar 18," said Cassandra. "But in all my air force training, it was barely mentioned except as a joke. It's not supposed to exist."

"It doesn't, as far as I know," said Luke.

"Not officially," said Ariella, as she led them around the rear of the building to a long annex. They followed the exterior of the annex to an enormous, unmarked hangar behind it. "They have a different name for it now. It's not important. What's important is what's inside."

Luke didn't even bother asking her what the new name was. He'd heard the legends about Hangar 18. Allegedly, materials from the 1947 Roswell UFO crash had been transported there for research. The military, of course, denied its existence, but anecdotes from military personnel had made it to the press, and the rumors took off from there. Nothing would surprise him.

Ariella led them to a small, unassuming metal door that was on the side of the hangar. Hargrove, Brody, and the others were gazing up nervously at the copters, which still hovered overhead. Luke couldn't see the ground forces anymore. He could imagine the dialogue as they scrambled to come up with a plan.

"It's inside," said Ariella. "It's been calling to me."

"Whatever it is, we better hurry," he said. "This is gonna escalate fast."

Ariella opened the door and went inside. Luke was the first one in behind her. Immediately, he marveled at the sheer size of the hangar. It was massive, much larger than it appeared from the outside. The entire hangar was empty, except for an old World War II plane in the center.

"That's a B-17 Flying Fortress!" said Cassandra. "There aren't many of those left."

"I hope we're not making our getaway in *that*," said Brody.

"I doubt it's even airworthy," said Cassandra. "Only eight of them are, to my knowledge."

A grinding noise startled Luke. The plane began moving sideways. That's when he realized, the floor beneath the plane was moving. He looked over at Ariella, who didn't seem surprised at all.

"Are *you* doing this?" he said.

"You'd be surprised how many things are hidden under your feet," she said, as the floor continued to slide open. He noticed the hinges where the floor was sliding, so Ariella must've activated an already-existing secret compartment.

"I'll be damned," said Hargrove, looking down into the gradually expanding gap.

"What the..." said Brody, his voice tailing off.

Luke looked down as well and his mouth dropped. As the floor slid open, the massive subterranean platform was revealed underneath. And in the center rested what could only be described as an alien spaceship, unless it was the most advanced flying vehicle ever built by man. It was about the size of a Boeing 747, a shiny, white, triangular object with curved edges and no apparent windows or doors. While triangular in shape, the object had nothing that could be described as wings and didn't even appear to be aerodynamically designed. It looked more like something from a modern art museum.

"Come," said Ariella, as she descended a flight of stairs that were built into the floor.

Luke and the others followed her. Luke was really wishing he'd had his backpack about now, but at least Hargrove, Martinez, and Cassandra had theirs.

As he descended the metal steps, he marveled at the extraordinary, sleek vehicle. It didn't appear damaged in the slightest, though how anyone would get in it was anyone's guess. More importantly, how did it come to be in the U.S. Air Force's possession? Was it given to them? Was it found after a crash? If so, how long ago? A million questions flooded his mind.

Like a schoolboy in a candy store, he rushed ahead to the ship. He brushed his hands along the shiny white object, well aware of the importance of the moment. He was touching something that likely traversed galaxies. This couldn't have been man-made. As an experiment, he took his keys out of his pocket and lightly scratched a key against the side of the ship. The surface remained perfectly smooth. He scratched harder. Again, no impact. He banged on the surface. There was no echo or give. It felt as solid as a boulder, yet the material resembled fiberglass.

"This shouldn't be able to fly," said Cassandra, coming up beside him.

"It doesn't even dent," said Luke.

Ariella approached the ship and placed a hand on the side of it. Instantly, a large door silently slid open, though there was no sign of any cracks or door frames. A small ramp extended automatically.

"Mother of God!" said Hargrove.

"Not quite," said Ariella.

"Do you know what this ship is?" said Luke.

"It's Alaktian," she said. "From my father's fleet. Follow me."

He followed her up the ramp and inside, and the others did the same.

"How did it get here?" he said.

"I don't know," she said. "I only know it's here."

"Wow, there's something she doesn't know," said Brody. "By the way, is this safe? We're not gonna end up in space or something, are we?"

"Hey, there aren't any seats," said Royster.

Luke noticed it, too. The ship was surprisingly empty inside. In fact, it was completely empty, as shiny and sleek inside as out. The interior was illuminated, yet there were no signs of any lights.

Ariella waved her hand again and a huge image of a control panel appeared on the ship's inner wall. Luke didn't recognize any of the symbols. The icons almost looked like Sumerian cuneiform script, which he recalled from his course in Ancient Languages. Except this was different altogether. She seemed to be selecting options just by looking at them, without actually touching anything. Immediately, the perimeter of the ship's interior turned translucent, revealing the external platform they had entered from.

Luke got startled when the ship appeared to rise, hovering in mid-air, though he couldn't feel any movement.

"What's happening?" said Brody, sounding more than a

little concerned.

"Why don't I feel anything?" said Luke, surprised to still be standing. "Is this a simulation?"

"It's a controlled gravitational environment," she said, turning toward him. "You won't feel us moving."

"Incredible," said Cassandra.

Ariella turned her head again toward the control panel and a list of symbols appeared.

"Just as I thought," she said.

"What?" said Luke.

"The ship was last operated sixty-two years ago. It must've been abandoned and brought here. I doubt your scientists have made any progress since then."

"*Our* scientists?" said Brody. "Now she's starting to scare me."

Before Luke could even comment, the ship suddenly ascended rapidly, crashing through the ceiling and spinning as they rose high in the air. As they whizzed above the copters, Luke caught a quick glimpse of the astonished expression on one of the airmen's faces—he looked like a cat mesmerized by a laser light. Indeed, the ship moved as if gravity didn't matter.

"Does somebody want to tell me how we're still standing?" said Hargrove, who appeared as shocked as Luke was.

"Ariella, how is this possible?" said Cassandra.

"It's hard to explain," said Ariella. "The system recognizes forces of bodily mass and adjusts the field around you accordingly. Try to fall. You won't be able to."

Luke tried to lean back. It was like an invisible pillow was keeping him from doing so. He couldn't lean forward either. Yet, he could walk, with some extra effort against the resistance. It felt like walking in a swimming pool. He could see the others trying to do the same. Just then, the ship instantly darted above the clouds in a matter of seconds, before racing forward at hypersonic speed. If he didn't know better, he would've thought he was watching it on TV, or that it was merely a simulation.

"This is mind-boggling," said Martinez.

"That girl," said Hargrove, "is something else."

Luke glanced over at Ariella, astounded at the remarkable increase in her knowledge and maturity. She'd always been wise beyond her years, but it was like she turned into an advanced adult being practically overnight, yet still in a child's body.

"We'll be arriving at Death Valley in sixteen minutes," said Ariella.

"Sixteen minutes, huh," said Hargrove. "That's at least a four-hour flight by plane."

"Luckily, this isn't a plane," said Ariella.

"You coulda fooled me," said Brody.

"Currently, we're traveling 8,500 miles an hour, or 2.3 miles per second."

"Per second!?" said Hargrove.

"Doesn't feel like it," said Royster.

"That's over Mach 11!" said Cassandra.

"Take that, Tom Cruise," said Brody.

"It goes much faster," said Ariella.

"No!" said Brody. "This is fast enough."

Luke paced slowly, his legs feeling like lead weights. He couldn't believe how quickly the ship was moving and yet from what it felt like, they may as well have been standing still. He could see Hargrove and Martinez at the other end of the ship, also taking awkward steps while in deep discussion about something. Brody and Royster were staring out the integrated pseudo-window as the clouds whizzed by below.

Luke was just observing everyone when Cassandra came up and put an arm around him.

"What do you think about all this?" she said.

He smiled. "I think we'll be early."

"We can hide," said Ariella. "The ship has a cloaking device, which I've already activated. Nobody can see us."

"Not even Valdok?" said Luke.

"He already knows we're coming. He's ready for us."

"That's not good."

"No, it isn't," she said. It was the first time he'd really heard her unsure of herself, which didn't make him feel any better.

"You do realize the situation we're in," said Brody, interrupting their conversation. "The cat's out of the bag. The whole damn Air Force saw us escape in a spaceship. Whether anyone sees us or not, I'm afraid this is Custer's Last Stand."

"Not necessarily," said Ariella.

"How do you figure?"

Ariella's eyes narrowed. "Lieutenant Colonel George Custer had around seven hundred men in his regiment, which he stupidly split into three groups."

"How do you—"

"When Sitting Bull united the Sioux and Cheyenne tribes," she continued, "their combined numbers were more than ten thousand. Custer was grossly outnumbered."

"Well, aren't *we*?" said Brody.

"Not as much as you would be without me."

Luke smiled as Brody shook his head in disbelief. There was the confidence he knew and loved.

"Okay, let's say we do get lucky and win," said Brody, "I'm afraid the rest of our planet may not see things your way."

"If I'm able to do what I was born to do, then I'm sure the whole world will understand."

"Yeah, I hope you're right, cause there's a guy they call the Destroyer of Worlds who has a say in the matter."

CHAPTER 21

POWER REVEALED

Lance Kilgore was back in Valdok's ship, and his mind was going a mile a minute. He wasn't sure how his intimidating celestial host would react to the news that the girl was gone. He had no choice but to just blurt it out.

"We lost her," he said. "*I* lost her. She rescued them all. But you wouldn't believe wha—"

"Good," said Valdok, once again in the form of a silver-haired man.

"Good?"

"It is as I anticipated. Why do you think I had my ship intercept her and her group at that point in their journey? Why do you think it was that I had you secure her colleagues in that precise location?"

"You knew she'd come for them."

"I was counting on it."

"I thought you wanted to prevent her from arriving."

"Incorrect. I wanted to prevent her from interfering. Before, I was merely testing her power. And... your loyalty."

"But you don't understand," said Kilgore. "I—"

"Please," said Valdok. "Tell me what it is that *I* do not understand." Valdok was mocking him now.

Kilgore took a breath to not get worked up by Valdok's arrogance. "I *saw* her power. I saw what she did," he said, firmly. "She disabled a room full of trained operatives. Twisted their M4 rifles like they were bubble gum. Then she put up some kind of shield against a whole squadron of airmen, including two attack birds. I mean, she's not human at all. She doesn't even seem stoppable." He threw up his hands. "She took off in a damn spaceship. What can we do against something like that?"

"*You* can do nothing. *I*, on the other hand, can do everything."

He watched as Valdok seemed to grow in stature. It wasn't his imagination. Valdok *was* growing—and changing form as well. He stepped back a few feet as Valdok transformed and expanded, until he took the form of an eight-foot-tall humanoid with grey skin, an oversized head, and pointy teeth like a crocodile. His eyes were black, empty, and soulless—like the eyes of a shark about to chomp down on its victim.

Valdok held out an enormous hand. Kilgore immediately felt his own weapon, a 357 Magnum, being pulled out of his holster into thin air. He observed in awe as Valdok tweaked his hand and the weapon immediately turned to dust.

"The girl is a babe in the woods and overestimates her abilities," said Valdok, his voice now booming and echoing throughout the ship. "At every step, I have been dictating her moves. It was I who led her near the Alaktian ship. I sensed its presence. I knew she would be drawn to it as a calf to its mother. They are en route to the theater of operations at this very moment and even she does not realize her mistake. You see, they are in a flying Faraday cage, Mr. Kilgore. The spider, as they say on your feeble little planet, has caught the fly."

CHAPTER 22

DEATH VALLEY

The flight to Death Valley went by in a matter of minutes. Luke couldn't help but wonder what other remarkable sights around the universe the ship had seen. Out of the wraparound window, he could see endless miles of desert sand with jagged mountain peaks off in the distance. He held Cassandra's hand.

"It's beautiful," he said.

Cassandra shook her head and seemed preoccupied. "We have so much to learn," she said. "We're like infants in the great big universe—babes in the woods."

Luke thought of a line from Exodus and recited it out loud. "Who is like you, oh Lord, among the gods? Who is like you, majestic in holiness, awesome in glorious deeds, doing wonders?"

At once, the ship came to a stop in mid-air.

"Did that just happen?" said Cassandra.

"Good thing this isn't a plane or we'd all be jelly by now."

The ship then descended vertically in the same manner. Luke braced himself out of habit, but then felt his stomach, wondering why he didn't feel any of the expected butterflies as they plummeted. He smiled and looked at Cassandra, who was gazing back at him wide-eyed.

"I don't feel anything!" he said, laughing.

Ariella then manipulated the ship into such a quiet landing, it seemed as if it was hand-placed onto the sand, though it seemed they had landed in the middle of an endless array of dunes.

"Now *that's* the way to travel," said Brody.

"Nice landing," said Luke, feeling the gravitational control return to normal.

"Don't thank me," said Ariella. "Thank the ship."

Hargrove and Martinez were moving in place, getting their land legs back.

Royster approached and was about to say something, but a tremendous boom rattled Luke's bones and rocked everyone to the core. It came from outside. The windows, which were more like digital viewers, went dark. The ship itself was still illuminated inside.

"What was that!?" said Luke.

Ariella looked concerned. She darted her eyes around the control panel.

"None of the controls are working," she said. She looked up and closed her eyes. After a few seconds, she opened them again. "Something's wrong," she said. "I can't sense anything outside the ship."

"Okay, now I'm getting worried," said Brody.

Royster looked terrified.

Ariella looked at them calmly. "It must be Valdok. He's the only one who could do this."

Hargrove approached. "You did say you could beat this guy, right?"

"I said I stood a better chance than any of you."

"Ariella," said Luke, "If you can't sense anything outside

of the ship, does that mean Valdok can't sense you either?"

"I believe it does," she said. "That's not good, Luke."

"Wait a minute," said Brody. "How is that not good?"

"It means we're trapped in here. We can't do anything to stop him."

"Trapped for how long?" said Royster, who appeared to be sweating.

Ariella shook her head. "I don't know."

"Wait a minute," said Cassandra. "We're in a Faraday cage. I remember experimenting with them when I was an undergrad."

Hargrove crinkled his forehead. "And this is relevant why?"

"I'm not sure I follow, either," said Luke.

"A Faraday cage is any solid conductive container that's completely enclosed," said Cassandra, "so it can block electromagnetic fields in or out. In other words, this ship. If Valdok somehow sealed us in and disabled the controls, then that could theoretically block Ariella's ability to communicate."

"That makes as much sense as anything," said Luke, "but what do we do about it?" He could see Royster sitting on the floor against the wall with his head in his hands. He didn't look well.

"Does anyone have a compass?" said Cassandra.

"I do," said Hargrove. "It's in my backpack. I'll get it."

Luke watched as Hargrove went to his backpack and came running back holding a standard issue compass, which he knew to be the Model 3H Tritium Lensatic Compass. Hargrove handed it to her.

Cassandra studied at it as she turned around.

"Odd," she said. "It doesn't work. Usually, the earth's magnetic field varies slowly, so it can pass through a Faraday cage. I remember doing that experiment. This compass should work."

"It won't work here," said Ariella. "It's too much to explain. But I know what will."

"What?" said Cassandra.

"Gamma rays."

"Gamma rays!?" said Hargrove.

"I saw a play about that once," said Brody. "The Effect of Gamma Rays on Man-in-the-Moon Marigolds. I don't remember anything about it though. My wife dragged me there. God, I miss her."

Luke patted Brody on the back.

"Yes, gamma rays can pass through," said Ariella, ignoring Brody's comment. "You would need several inches of lead or a few feet of concrete to block them."

"It's why we wear lead aprons when we get x-rays," said Cassandra.

"How does that help us?" said Luke, looking at Ariella. "Can you... *use* gamma rays?"

"They're only high energy waves of a super-high frequency," said Ariella, as if everyone knew that. "I should be able to modulate my signal."

Luke watched as she approached the far wall of the ship and extended her arms forward. She placed her hands against the white material and turned her head.

"Stay as far back as you can," she said. "I'll try to control it."

"Ariella, wait," said Cassandra. "You don't have any protection from the radiation yourself."

"I don't need it, Mother. It'll be okay."

Cassandra turned to Luke. "I miss when she called me Mommy." Luke put his arm around her.

Ariella focused all her concentration on the wall of the ship. There was no rumbling, no vibrations, no mysterious glows—just silence. Everyone just stared at one another, wondering what was going on. Luke could hear his own heartbeat as he waited to see what would happen. Then he saw it—a faint glow on Ariella's sapphire-blue amulet.

Immediately, the side of the ship slid open, and a rush of hot air came inside. Luke could see nothing but desert sand outside the ship. He couldn't make out any of the surroundings. Royster made a mad dash for the door, but Hargrove grabbed him.

"Hold on there, Sergeant," said Hargrove. "You can't just go running out there like an anxious racehorse."

Just then, the door slid shut.

"Why did it close!?" said Royster. "Why did it close!?"

"It's not time yet," said Ariella. We'll leave when it's time."

Royster was sweating.

"Kevin," said Luke, "what's going on?"

Royster tried to catch his breath. "I—I'm claustrophobic, Luke. Ever since Afghanistan. I tried to manage it. Really, I did. But when our ship got blasted, it just brought me back, and—"

"I pulled you out of that, Kevin. And you'll survive this, too. Just like Afghanistan."

Royster nodded. "Just like Afghanistan," he repeated, though he didn't seem entirely convinced.

Luke felt a tug on the back of his shirt. He turned around. It was Ariella.

"Luke, I'm sorry," she said, once again seeming like a young girl.

"Sorry about what?"

"I feel like I ruined your life."

"Ruined my life?" he said. "Ariella, you saved my life. I had nothing after I lost my family. You know that."

"That's the thing," she said. "I feel like I may have caused that."

"Caused it!?" He was totally confused now. "Ariella,

Nathaniel Dixon caused that. He just went crazy. It was nobody else's fault. Probably not even his."

"I don't think Nathaniel Dixon just suddenly went crazy. I was looking for you around that same time, because I knew you were meant to help me. I can't help but think Valdok knew that and tried to kill you through Dixon. Except he got your family instead."

Luke thought about it and his heart sank. It made sense. If he had only left Dixon alone, Dixon would've killed him instead. His wife and daughter would still be alive. Still, it wasn't Ariella's fault, even if it *was* the case. She was as much a pawn in this as he was. Yes, that's what he felt like—a pawn, and he was tired of it. He tightened his fists, thinking once again about that horrific day. A million emotions flooded his head, but ultimately, it didn't change anything. As he returned his thoughts to the present and the mission at hand, the tension began to leave his body. He knelt in front of Ariella.

"Even if that's true," he said, "you didn't know. This is on Valdok, and we're gonna stop him. We'll do it in honor of Kathleen and Kayla."

She nodded.

He smiled. "They would've loved you."

A slight smile formed on Ariella's face for the first time in a while.

Over the next couple of hours, they all tried to stay calm and wait. They discussed everything from baseball stadiums to old sci-fi movies to their favorite cars. Luke's was an old, spruced-up Opel Manta his grandfather had given him. All the while, the specter of whatever awaited them would creep in, as they anxiously awaited the signal from Ariella that it was time to go. And whenever the room grew silent, Luke could sense the palpable fear in everyone's hearts.

Soon, hunger and thirst began to overtake the trepidation. Fortunately, Hargrove and Martinez still had their backpacks with snacks and several bottles of water, which everyone shared. Still, it wouldn't last long, and it wasn't enough even for now. Luke tried to think ahead about how to conserve for what could be a long ordeal. He recalled hearing in his training how Napoleon's multi-national troops ate their four-day food rations the first day in the ill-fated march to Russia—the first of many things to go wrong during that campaign.

Out of the corner of his eye, he noticed Ariella lift her hand and position her palm toward where the ship's door had opened and closed earlier. Her amulet, the sapphire blue An'za stone, began to glow. One by one, the others noticed, too. Then the door slid open.

"It's time," she said. "I'll go first."

As Luke felt the rush of warm air enter the ship, he wasn't sure what was worse, the waiting or the realization that they were now about to face the unknown.

"Wait a minute," said Royster. "We don't even have any weapons. They were confiscated back at—"

"Martinez and I do," said Hargrove.

"Well, good for you," said Royster, but that—"

"Let's get there first," said Ariella. "Then we'll worry about the weapons."

"This plan just keeps getting better," said Brody.

"You all need to have faith," said Ariella. "I told you we'd need to do scary things. We have no choice."

Royster nodded. "Well, okay then," he said, seeming to compose himself. He looked at Hargrove. "Admiral, I'm sorry for my outburst. I was having flashbacks of... well, it's not important."

"Sergeant," said Hargrove, "it's human to be afraid, to have doubts and trauma." He paused. "But, then you're not just a human, are you? You're a Marine. So, you know we can't go into a battle accepting defeat. And you know there's no greater honor than to fight for one another. Not a flag, not a country, not glory, not the Marine Corps—for each other—maybe for the whole planet. Duty before fear, son. *Honor* before fear. Now, you were given a second chance at life for a reason. I believe this is that reason. We may die today. But when I look at that little, amazing girl, I don't think we will. And if we do, well, that's what we're here for, you and I, isn't it?"

Luke could see Royster growing taller with each word Hargrove spoke.

"Now I think you have something else you want to say, Sergeant," said Hargrove.

"Oorah!" yelled Royster, without hesitation.

"Damn right," said Hargrove. "Let me hear that again."

"Oorah!"

"Now let's go kick some alien ass."

CHAPTER 23

THE SINGING SANDS

As Luke exited the ship into the arid desert terrain, he could feel the scorching heat singe his nostrils. He glanced around and realized the ship had settled on a plateau of a massive sand dune. The dunes to both sides of it were even higher, possibly at least five or six hundred feet high. It dawned on him that Ariella may have chosen the location strategically for cover, though Valdok must've somehow sensed they were there when he had sealed them inside the ship. Would he sense them now?

"Make sure you all have your necks covered," he said, remembering his training. "Pull your shirt over your head if you have to. The head's the most important thing to keep cool. As it is, we'll last maybe five miles tops walking in the heat of day. More if we can find shade."

Luke followed his own advice and pulled his t-shirt over his head. He gave his outer shirt to Cassandra to use as a scarf. Then they both stepped onto the sand and trudged ahead trying to keep up with Ariella. It was more difficult than he had expected. With each step forward it felt like he took a step back, as his feet kept sinking into the hot sand—especially as they approached an incline up ahead, toward the peak of the dune. The others were having similar difficulties, and a few took the occasional tumble. With the SEALS, he'd gone through extensive training in all terrains, including desert battles, but hadn't experienced anything quite like this and in this degree of heat. There was a big difference between drills in the desert and what he was now traversing through.

"Are we having fun yet?" said Hargrove, huffing and puffing.

"I feel like Ben Hur," said Brody. "Where's Jesus?"

"I hope we find him before he finds us," said Royster.

"I mean *real* Jesus," said Brody. "Didn't you ever see Ben Hur?"

As they followed Ariella up the dune, Luke could hear a low hum that gradually grew louder until it sounded like a deep choir—as if a hundred pipe organs were playing at once.

"Is that Valdok's ship making that sound?" he asked Ariella.

Martinez answered first, coming up from behind. "No, it's the dunes. The Singing Sands." He took a breath. "We're in the Eureka Sand Dunes, just like I said. Look." He pointed to the large, majestic dune to the right. "As the sand slides down the steep face of the dune, it makes that sound. It's coming from the other side, too. It's beautiful, isn't it?"

"Like the horns of Jericho," said Luke. The irony wasn't lost on him. He thought back to the first time he'd read the biblical story of Joshua, who'd led the Israelites into the Battle of Jericho. Seven priests in the presence of the Lord blew seven ram's horns, causing the walls to crumble and allowing a great victory to the Israelites. Little did he know he'd one day be in an equally supernatural battle—except this time led by a young girl against a false god. Two-thousand years from now, would anyone believe it? That is, if there was anyone left to believe anything.

The group continued, and occasionally they would pause for Hargrove to pass around a water bottle or two for them to share. The water had to be running out by now, but as Luke learned in training, it was better to store water in your body than in a canteen. Water rationing was a myth when it came to the desert. The name of the game was to lose as little water as possible.

"Breathe through your nose," Hargrove said to the group, probably reading his mind. "You lose less water than way."

It felt like they were walking for half a day, but it was probably only about an hour. Time has a habit of standing still when you're trekking through a seemingly infinite desert in the scorching heat. All along, the magical choir of the sands had been resonating throughout the dunes, but occasionally they would grow quiet, as they did now, and make way for the desert wind.

"Stop," said Ariella, pausing as they finally came to the peak of the dune. "I can see them."

"See who?" said Royster and Martinez, almost in unison.

Luke stepped up beside her. Hargrove joined and looked through a pair of standard-issue binoculars he must've had in his bag.

"U.S. Army," said Hargrove. "Our best and brightest and lots of them. Must be a few hundred thousand civilians down there, too. Looks like a pretty well-planned crowd containment operation."

"Almost as if they were in on it," said Luke, not hiding his sarcasm.

"I guarantee you they know a lot less than we do, so let's cut them some slack," said Hargrove.

The deep choir of the sands resumed, as if to foreshadow the danger to come.

"Any sign of Valdok?" said Cassandra.

"Negative," said Hargrove.

"He's here," said Ariella. "I sense him. And the Karn are above us. In the skies."

Luke looked up but saw nothing but clouds. He had almost forgotten the name of Valdok's race of scavengers.

"It looks like Woodstock down there," said Brody.

"Three days of peace and music," said Royster, who, like Luke, was clearly too young to remember the concert, but had probably seen the posters.

"More like blood and aliens," said Brody.

"Lieutenant Brody is correct," said Ariella.

"Hell, I hope not!" snapped Brody. "It wasn't a prediction."

Luke borrowed Hargrove's binoculars to get a better look. He scanned the area. This was indeed well-coordinated. It was clear that the military was fully aware of what would be transpiring, when, and where—as the crowd was expertly facilitated into organized sections. What was less clear was whether they were aware of the full story. Likely they weren't, as Hargrove had said. He followed the line of soldiers around the perimeter of the crowd. As he moved from right to left with his binoculars, he came upon a soldier with a huge pair of military binoculars—aimed straight at him.

"Shit," said Luke.

"What?" said Cassandra.

"They see us."

He froze as he spotted a whole group of soldiers leave their posts, weapons aimed in their direction. The first barrage of fire from the army's long-range weapons barely missed them.

"Get down!" said Luke, as everyone fell to the sand.

"I figured we'd be on a watch list," said Hargrove. "What's Plan B?"

"There is no Plan B," said Ariella. "We're still on my plan."

"This is your plan?" said Brody.

"They'll be up here in no time," said Hargrove.

"We need to go meet them," said Ariella.

"Little girl, I don't understand your strategy at all," said Hargrove.

She rose nonchalantly and began descending the dune. Luke was about to protest, but then he remembered how she had protected them at Wright-Patterson when they were taking fire. But this would likely escalate to a whole new scale. Putting his faith in Ariella, he nodded to the others as he stood.

No sooner had they begun their descent than more soldiers came, firing a relentless stream of ammunition. Ariella held up a hand and Luke could hear the sound of bullets being redirected to the left. The low hum of the dunes provided a haunting background chorus to the battle.

The group continued behind Ariella as the soldiers began to climb, still firing—the sound of repeated ammo growing louder and louder. But it was something Luke spotted down below that alarmed him more. Four army men were wheeling into place what looked like a howitzer, but more futuristic. He could see the bright sun reflecting off the shiny silver. Was it some sort of reverse-engineered alien tech?

He tapped Ariella on the shoulder and shouted over the noise of the gunfire and the dunes. "What do you think that is!?"

She shrugged her shoulders. It didn't make him feel any better.

He turned to Hargrove. "Ever see anything like that?"

Hargrove looked through his binoculars. "Hell, no. That's not one of ours."

"Still think we should cut them some slack?"

"Live first, think later," said Hargrove, motioning to back up as the howitzer pointed in their direction.

On instinct, Luke shouted to the others to get back, as he

watched them dive out of sight and then joined them. He looked up to see Ariella still standing.

"Get down!" he said.

"I have to focus, Luke," she said without turning. He hoped she knew what she was up against.

The bullets still kept coming, and each time they were easily misdirected by Ariella. Then the choir of the sands dissipated, and a strange, new noise took its place, this time from down below—a shrill, high-pitched hum, building in power.

Luke rose just enough to see what was going on. Ariella was still standing. He climbed to his feet and stood behind her. That's when he spotted a bright glow coming from the howitzer-like weapon.

"Down!" he shouted to Ariella.

"Quiet, Luke," she said, as if he was interrupting her TV show.

At once, a bright ray of light shot toward them with a shriek. It was upon them in an instant. He watched as Ariella held both of her palms toward the beam. Her An'za amulet was glowing brightly. Sparks burst forth from the powerful clash of energy—hers against the weapon's. He could see she was struggling. The pressure appeared to be building up until the super-howitzer down below exploded with a tremendous, deafening blast. The four soldiers operating it never stood a chance. When the smoke and sand cleared, there was nothing left of them.

Ariella and whatever mysterious force was helping her had won this round, but there was a larger battle yet to be fought against a much more powerful enemy.

Civilians began to panic down below, the surrounding soldiers firing in the air to get the crowd under control. The soldiers continued to climb up the dune, continuously firing round after round. They didn't seem like they had any intention of giving up, nor would he if he were in their situation. They were trained not to give up. To take the hill no matter what.

Luke could see from her red face that Ariella was angry. She threw her hands in disgust and the whole squadron of armed soldiers went flying backward down the dune, their weapons thrown in all directions.

She turned to Luke. "Let's get down there," she said.

The others rose, and Luke and Ariella led the way. He let Ariella take the lead as Cassandra caught up.

"I'm worried, Luke," said Cassandra.

"I think we all are. We're in uncharted territory here." He kept a close eye on his footing on the uneven sand.

"No, I mean for Ariella. I realize she has all these powers, but she's still my daughter, and this was just one weapon she had to face. I'm not ready to lose her."

"Cass, nobody on Earth has been in your situation. I mean not unless you count Mother Mary. But you couldn't stop her if you tried. She's on a mission, and we have to have faith that she's fulfilling her purpose. If anyone can get through this, she can. We have to believe she's gonna get us through this."

"I sure hope you're right."

"Remember, she's gotten us out of everything so far. Surprised us every time. And she's only getting stronger. By the minute it seems." He pointed to the scattered bodies and weapons ahead of them.

"So far, she's been battling humans. I saw what a hard time she had in the car with Valdok getting in her head."

"Well let's hope she's stronger now."

Cassandra took his hand and they descended the dune trying to keep up with Ariella. Down below, a new unit of soldiers had their weapons aimed at them, while the rest kept the masses under control. They knew better than to fire quite yet. They were no doubt awaiting instructions.

Just as Luke and the group marched with Ariella into the

awaiting valley and toward the new squadron of soldiers, a burst of light appeared in the sky. A figure descended slowly from the clouds right down into the center of the crowd. The people frantically moved back to make way, jostling one another for position, some tripping onto the scorching sand. They began shouting at one another.

Valdok was back in his Christ-like form as he stretched out his open arms, the sleeves of his white robe dangling from each arm like Victorian drapes. As he stood in the clearing made by the crowd, he gazed directly at Ariella, then around at the bystanders. The throngs grew quiet.

"Blessed are all of you," Valdok began, his voice echoing throughout the valley, "who have shown faith this day of transcendence. For you shall be rewarded."

People began kneeling, and it spread like a wave, even amongst a number of the soldiers, who laid down their arms.

"Your painless ascent to the great kingdom is my gift to the faithful. Safe from the fires and the venom that shall soon spout forth with a great reckoning. Come take your place with your loved ones and live together in glory. The Kingdom of Heaven awaits all of you!"

The clouds grew dark up ahead. Something was happening in the skies.

"You're a false god, Valdok!" yelled Ariella, whose voice also resonated throughout the valley. "Tell them who you really are. The Destroyer of Worlds."

The crowd began murmuring again as people turned toward Ariella.

"Behold," said Valdok, quieting the people. "The spawn of the devil speaks with a foul tongue. But the devil's child has no dominion over any of you, just as her father had no dominion over me."

Valdok sneered at Ariella. Luke glanced over at her. Clearly that was a dig against Kersius, her real father, no doubt meant to rile her up. The young girl remained unphased.

Valdok redirected his attention to his minions.

"It is time to cast away demons," he said. "Witness the power of *my* Father above!"

A burst of thunder startled everyone, and flashes of lightning appeared in the clouds. Immediately, a massive beam of powerful energy came down directly at Ariella. Once again, she held her hands above her head and dug her feet into the sand. Her amulet glowed. Again, it was power against power as she held steadfast against the uncompromising death ray. Luke could see her straining to hold her ground. It was clear she was having a harder time than with the howitzer. Never had he felt so helpless. He didn't even have a weapon and there was a whole army unit behind him ready to shoot him down if he tried anything. He turned to Cassandra and the others, who clearly felt as powerless as he did. He grasped Cassandra's hand tightly.

After what seemed like minutes, the beam from above finally dissipated. Ariella stood tall.

"He is Valdok the Destroyer," she said to the crowd. "And he did not come here to save any of you, but to take you. Above those clouds is a fleet of his spaceships."

"Turn your eyes and ears from the devil's temptations," said Valdok to the crowd. "A leviathan in a young girl's body spits venom to baffle the herd, but I am the good shepherd, and I will not lead you astray. Remain steadfast as you kneel. Divert your eyes to the ground and prepare to enter the greatest realm of all."

"He's lying to you all," shouted Ariella. "Leave now, while you can."

Luke scanned the crowd as everyone began murmuring. Some people looked confused, as if they didn't know which party to believe. Others were trembling in fear of the unknown. Some soldiers were kneeling. Others were standing at the ready, not sure what would be required of them at any moment.

The skies began rumbling.

"This," said Valdok, "is the power of the Lord. Behold!"

Ariella gazed at the skies and held a palm up as she grasped her An'za stone with the other hand. The clouds began to part.

"Behold Valdok's fleet," she said to the crowd.

The people collectively gasped, and those who'd been looking down were now staring up at the skies.

Slowly the clouds parted, revealing an enormous oval spacecraft the size of a football field. Luke could see two rows of green lights circling around the perimeter. Then the adjacent clouds began to dissipate, revealing another oval ship, and another. The others were smaller than the mothership, but still imposing—each one at least twice the size of a commercial airliner. The ships remained eerily still and silent, as if wind or gravity had no impact.

"They're race is the Karn," said Ariella. "And they want to take the planet."

People began to panic. Even Luke was shocked. There had to be at least twenty or thirty ships filling the skies for as far as he could see. Wide swaths of beams came down and people began getting sucked up into the air by the dozens. The crowd began screaming and running, while the military tried to control the turmoil. Then even the soldiers began backing up.

"The child plays trickery to deceive you!" said Valdok, though as he surveyed the crowd it was clear he'd lost his grasp over his audience. Valdok knew it, and now all bets were off. Valdok stood tall and smiled, not seeming the least bit concerned. What was he up to?

Luke watched in horror as evil deceiver began to rapidly grow in stature. In front of the terrified crowd, he shed his robes and transformed into a giant humanoid creature with grey skin and an enormous head, with pointy, jagged teeth and black eyes. He had to be nearly ten feet tall.

The soldiers began firing into the sky at the ships, trying to avoid hitting the countless people being sucked up into them. Some fired at Valdok, to no avail. Ariella stepped forward as Valdok jerked his head toward her and snarled. But Ariella wasn't looking at him. She was looking up.

Luke followed her gaze to see hundreds of alien creatures similar to Valdok descending from the ships, firing rays at the soldiers.

The Karn invasion had begun.

CHAPTER 24

THE DOME

Luke watched as Ariella yelled, "Run!" to the crowd, her voice echoing as she stood firm to face the enemy. She motioned for Luke and the others to stay behind her.

People scurried desperately in all directions to escape the area. Almost immediately, an enormous dome—it appeared to be some kind of semi-transparent energy barrier—came down from the Karn ships and formed all around the throng. They were all trapped. Families banged and clawed at the invisible wall trying to escape. Soldiers and aliens fired at one another, with the aliens clearly gaining the edge with their advanced weaponry as they descended to the ground.

Ariella waved her arm, and a number of weapons were immediately pulled from the aliens' hands and catapulted across the air until they landed in front of Luke.

"Use them," she said.

Luke quickly handed weapons to the group, though he was still unsure what to do with them. He didn't even see a trigger.

"They're particle beam weapons," said Ariella, turning quickly. "Put your hand behind the squishy thing and squeeze."

"Squishy thing!?" said Brody from behind.

A barrage of beams came their way and Ariella blocked them with what looked like a translucent energy shield that sparkled around the edges.

"Can we shoot through your shield?" said Luke.

"Yes," she said. "I reversed the… it's too hard to explain. Just shoot!"

Luke stuck his hand in what felt like a pile of goo and put his fingers around some kind of joystick. It was pliable and he squeezed. A blast left his weapon and nearly threw him backward. But he took out two aliens at once with it.

"I think this'll do," he said.

As Ariella waved her hands around like an orchestra conductor, the semi-transparent shields appeared everywhere, some protecting Luke and the group, and others protecting as many soldiers as she could. Still, soldiers were dropping at alarming speed. People were being hurled into the air toward the ships by the hundreds. Perhaps twenty or thirty aliens had landed behind Luke's group—more importantly, behind the shields. It seemed even with Ariella, this was looking dire.

Luke turned to Cassandra. "Cass, protect yourself. Head back to the ship," he said. "Ariella can't afford to lose you. I'll cover you."

She shook her head. "Not a chance. I can't afford to lose her either."

"Are you sure you're okay firing weapons?"

She smirked at him and redirected her attention, taking out six aliens behind her in quick succession.

"I was the best shot in my unit during OTS combat training," she said.

"I can believe it," he said, more than a little impressed.

He spotted Hargrove and Martinez firing away at the still descending alien targets as if they were born using these strange weapons. Then one of the Karn snuck up behind and was about to attack them. Luke aimed to shoot it, but someone beat him to it. It was Brody, who then turned and took out two more Karn. Luke returned to taking out as many of them as he could, but it was getting hard to keep up. One blast nearly got him from behind, but Royster had tackled him and knocked him out of the way. Somehow, neither of them got hit.

"Looks like we're even," he said to Royster, as they both got up and continued their fire.

He glanced over at Ariella. She was doing the best she could, but soldiers continued to fall. She couldn't protect them all.

As he took out one target after another, Luke spotted Valdok ahead. He was hard to miss, as he stood a good foot or two above the other aliens. Valdok appeared to be manipulating the ships up above somehow as he reached up with his massive arms. He grinned an evil grin as he stared right at Luke and Ariella. Luke didn't waste any time. He took a shot directly at the smiling devil, but it had no impact.

Just then a high-pitched hum pierced the air from above as a whole array of powerful beams shot down from multiple Karn ships at once. They were all directed toward Ariella. She held up her hands to defend against them. He could see she was struggling to combat the searing death rays blasting down from the ships. Her forehead crinkled and her face grew red as she strained to keep her shield up. Her sapphire amulet glowed brightly as she continued to hold both hands up fending off the massive power blasts thrust against her. Luke could see sparks where her shield met the rays, and the sound grew louder, like the loud hum of a high voltage transformer.

Then his heart sank as he watched Ariella's knees fall to the ground as she struggled to stay upright. Meanwhile, the battle between the soldiers and the Karn continued around them.

Fortunately, Cassandra and the others in their group had effectively taken care of the Karn behind them, but the fight was far from over. He was grateful that Ariella's shields had been able to protect them from the front for the most part, but then he jumped as a soldier right next to him took a blast to the chest and fell. That's when he realized... Ariella's shields were down—all except for the one remaining shield she managed to conjure with one hand to protect herself.

He and Cassandra resumed firing away with a vengeance. He took out about six Karn in quick succession.

"We have to keep fighting!" he yelled. "Shields are down!" He spotted Hargrove, Martinez, Brody, and Royster all engaged in heavy combat, dodging blasts while they kept shooting.

"Shields are down!" he yelled to the others. He redirected his attention to Valdok and aimed his weapon again at the giant behemoth. Perhaps if he could just distract him. He fired the plasma weapon and kept firing. Valdok looked at him and snarled before returning his attention to the beams.

He glanced over at Ariella. Slowly, she was able to rise again and he could see in her face she was determined. He may have distracted Valdok just enough to give her a second wind.

Just then, he saw one of the Karn creatures rushing toward her from behind, weapon aimed directly at her. Luke wasn't close enough to push her out of the way and didn't even have time to turn and aim his weapon. So he did the only thing he could. He had no other choice.

Luke realized at that moment why he was needed here. Why he *had* to be here. It wasn't just because of his expert shooting skills or his SEAL training. This, in the end, was his purpose. Ariella might have known it all along but couldn't tell him. Or perhaps she didn't know. All of these thoughts flooded his head in the split second between life and death.

He jumped in the path of the Karn just as the alien took

the shot. He timed it so he'd take the full brunt of the blast. This was the mission, the most important mission in Earth's history—to protect Ariella.

He heard the sound of the blast and watched in slow motion as the deadly particle beam headed toward his chest. In a second, he would feel pain no more. He would have no control over the remaining events of the battle. His job will have been done.

He braced for the impact. He wondered if he would see Kathleen and Kayla. He hoped so.

He closed his eyes. No time to worry. Only to die.

♦

Luke fell to the ground. He was shaken and groggy, but the battle was still going on around him. He felt his chest. Somehow, he wasn't hit. Not even a scratch. He felt a hand on his shoulder and turned to see Ariella standing and facing the alien.

"Move," she said.

Luke shifted to the side and Ariella quickly lifted her hand. Immediately, a forceful blast of energy burst forth from her palm that completely disintegrated the surprised Karn.

Luke picked himself off the ground slowly. "Thanks for blocking that shot," he said. "Thought I was a goner there."

"That wasn't me, Luke," she said, returning her attention to the battle and raising all the shields once again. "Keep shooting."

"You mean y—" He paused, wondering what could have happened. Then he glanced quickly to the sky and nodded, smiling. Because surely a miracle had just happened.

His joy was short-lived.

The ships once again fired their combined rays toward Ariella—even stronger this time. Valdok was orchestrating the whole thing from below. Once again, she tried to defend herself. It seemed more Karn ships had joined in. It was becoming too much, even for her, and Valdok seemed to be rejoicing in it.

Destiny was a fickle thing. What seemed all but assured was now looking less certain. Luke felt an uneasiness in the pit of his stomach, but he knew he had to have faith. He glanced over at the others, still fighting fiercely. Brody, Royster, Hargrove, Martinez, and Cassandra. Heroes all. Martinez had taken a blast to the arm, but it hadn't slowed him down any. Cassandra and Brody were firing up at the ships, to no avail. Luke joined them, hoping their combined fire might make a difference.

"Aim at Valdok," he yelled over to them, figuring they could mimic the way the ships were all targeting Ariella. They collectively shifted their targets to the Karn leader. He swatted the blasts away like flies.

"Keep fighting!" he yelled to Ariella. "We're not going to lose today!"

That's when a blast hit Brody and he went down.

Just then, a huge explosion filled the air. Luke nearly jumped out of his skin. It seemed to be coming from beyond the ships. The beams directed at Ariella had stopped.

In the distance, he saw a Karn ship fall from the sky. Then another.

Luke gazed up into the clouds to see what was going on. Beyond the fleet of Karn ships, in between the clouds, he could see another fleet of ships enter the picture. They resembled the one he and the others had arrived in—a more angular shape than those of the Karn.

"It's my father," said Ariella. "It's Kersius."

"Gideon?" said Cassandra. "But I thought..."

"Apparently not," said Luke, smiling. "Looks like we have help." He turned to tend to Brody, but he couldn't find him anywhere.

Some of Kersius's ships began firing at the Karn on the ground while others targeted the Karn vessels.

Then a squadron of military jets arrived from behind them, some American and others Israeli. Elli Hassan must've come through.

"It's Elli," he said to Cassandra. "He must've gotten through to Kersius."

"Or the other way around," she said.

He glanced around again. "Have you seen Brody?"

"No," she said, as she resumed firing at the Karn.

He scanned around for Brody but didn't see him. Another blast came his way. Then another. The battle wasn't over quite yet. He lifted his weapon and took out a few more Karn. One particle beam came right at him but fell harmlessly to the ground. It seemed the shields were back up.

He glanced over at Ariella. Her An'za stone began glowing brighter than ever. He watched in wonder as she closed her eyes, as if meditating. Then she spread her arms out in a slow, graceful wave, the way a bird might spread its wings.

The dome lifted with a whirring sound. Immediately, many in the crowd began to flee. Some stayed to witness the events, hoping to see a great victory.

At once, the Karn creatures began dropping like flies. All except Valdok, who was now marching toward Ariella, not to be stopped. Soldiers fired at him, to no avail. Kersius's ships rained their blasts down on him, again with no impact.

Valdok the Destroyer was on a mission. It was to be him against Ariella, and it appeared nothing would get in his way.

Ariella stood firm to face him.

The young girl closed her eyes and raised her arms and the Karn bodies began to rise in the air. All the fallen weapons and dead American soldiers began to rise as well. The civilians and soldiers who remained in the path were also now floating in the air. Somehow, Ariella was creating a zero-gravity field around her and her enemy. Yet the two of them remained firmly on the ground. Luke wondered what she was playing at. At any rate, she appeared more powerful than ever.

Luke and the others stepped back. There was nothing anyone could do here accept Ariella.

"The Alaktian savior will finally meet her demise," said Valdok, his voice thundering throughout the valley. "And so will the humans. You have failed not one, but two races today."

"I'm still here to defend against your evil, Valdok," said Ariella, defiantly. "And I *will* defend this planet."

"This planet? You're not even of this world. These pitiful vermin who wish to believe in their silly dogma. They will not see heaven this day. But you might." He grinned a devious grin.

Luke felt his heart pounding as the nine-year-old girl faced the imposing colossus—the seemingly unstoppable godlike being that had decimated planets for millennia. Curiously, she seemed to be doing something with her hands as the Destroyer raised his arms to strike her. She was conjuring a small flame, which whirled around until it quickly grew into a pillar of fire. All the other objects and bodies in their path were still floating in mid-air.

"You wish to do battle with the elements," said Valdok. "A futile and unimpressive gesture."

Valdok conjured an enormous amount of sand and formed it into a tremendous wave to put out the fire, but the sand particles dispersed harmlessly into the zero-gravity air.

"Spawn of Alaktu," he said, trying to control the sands. "This world will fall like yours. You waste your time for this insignificant species. To think they believed I would send them all to their beloved heaven. They will *never* reach it."

"Maybe, not, Valdok," said Ariella. She paused as her face

grew red. Luke could see she was getting angrier by the second. "But I'm sending *you* to hell!" She threw her hands forward with such a fury that the fire began to engulf Valdok. His deathly and bloodcurdling howl of pain echoed throughout the valley as his face began to melt. She kept circling her hands as an air pocket formed around the Destroyer, trapping him in the flames. Then she brought her hands down slowly and all the people and dead bodies began lowering to the ground. The blazing fire dissipated, leaving nothing but a small pile of smoking cinders on the sand. Valdok, it seemed, was gone.

The small girl lowered her hands. The deafening cheer from hundreds of thousands of people came immediately. Hardened soldiers had tears in their eyes. Luke and Cassandra immediately ran to Ariella and put their arms around her. The girl's soft and fragile skin belied the powerful being she had just shown to be. She looked up at them and smiled, as if she'd just won a spelling bee.

Hargrove and Martinez came to congratulate her. But then Ariella grew more serious and shifted her gaze toward the field. Weary people cried for their loved ones who'd been taken, and soldiers mourned for the dead and tried to help those who were left.

"My job isn't finished yet," she said. "I have something else I have to do."

CHAPTER 25

REVELATION

L uke watched with Cassandra as Ariella stepped forward
into the desert valley. Many of those who had fled had
now returned. The crowd of people and soldiers alike
gathered around her, some cheering and many too shaken and
exhausted to cheer.

"I wish to say something," she said as the crowd grew
quiet. "The president and Special Agent Lance Kilgore are up
in those ships above us. They and the Chairman of the Joint
Chiefs of Staff made a deal with the Karn. A secret deal."

People began murmuring and then quieted down as she
scanned the crowd. They were probably also surprised to hear
such an eloquent child. Luke still had trouble getting used to
it.

"They had an agreement," she continued, "that all of those
here today would be taken by the Karn as slaves in exchange
for advanced technology."

Many in the crowd began yelling at the soldiers among
them.

"The soldiers here were not aware of this plan," she said.

"Neither was the Vice President or the Chief of Staff. And nobody, not even the president or Special Agent Kilgore knew about the other part of Valdok's plan."

She waited until everyone grew quiet, which they quickly did.

"After he took the slaves he needed, Valdok's plan was to eliminate the rest of humanity and take this world for his own. It's what he does. It's what he did to my father's world."

Luke knew how people would react. Some were silently shocked, and others gasped and backed away in fear. The soldiers stood firm and tried to keep everyone calm.

Then everyone grew immediately silent and seemed to be looking past Ariella. Luke directed his attention to the target of their gaze.

Through the dust of the sands, a throng of people were approaching from where the ships had fallen. At least he hoped they were people. As they got closer, he could see a figure leading them. A tall, thin, fortyish man wearing a blue and silver uniform. It was Kersius, this time here in the flesh. Elli Hassan was beside him. Nearby was Admiral Wilcox and several other senior officers. They had the president and Kilgore in handcuffs.

"My father arrives with those who were taken from you," said Ariella.

People began running toward their approaching loved ones, frantically searching for their families. Others stood back and cheered, their hails of ecstasy echoing throughout the valley.

Kersius approached Ariella and embraced her. He looked at Cassandra and smiled. Then he addressed the crowd as he stood next to his daughter. He waited silently for them to quiet down.

"My name is Kersius," he said.

There was a hush among the people, though many were

still searching for or hugging their loved ones.

"I come from a world near what you call Proxima Centauri. As you can see, we look very much like you, only twenty thousand years or so older as a race." He smiled, perhaps to reassure them.

"The universe is full of many races and creeds. We are not all your enemies. Nor are we all your friends. Many of us would look human to you, such as those in my world. The survivors of twelve worlds like mine have joined me here today to put an end to the Karn, who've ravaged our worlds for millennia. We have come to you in an act of goodwill and with our mutual interests in mind. My world is called Alaktu. In fact, my daughter, who you've met today, is half-Alaktian and half-human, born to serve as a defender against the evil you witnessed here today. I leave your world in her quite capable hands as we return to rebuild ours."

Many in the crowd nodded. Some were smiling. Some were crying.

"But I also leave you with a warning."

Luke glanced around as a wave of shocked faces spread across the throng. Every soul in the desert valley was now paying attention.

"It is more important than ever," said Kersius, "that you desist from your petty squabbles, power struggles, and wars over territory and resources. Move away from harsh judgement and toward empathy and understanding. Turn conflict into conversation. Heal your planet. And have a strong global police force to eliminate violence. If you do not, then there will come a time—and it could come sooner rather than later—that the Earth will no longer be subject to the care of humans."

The crowd collectively gasped.

"There are those far more powerful than I who would see it as a necessary corrective action, despite our collective agreement to let you evolve. Many of them are living on your planet as I speak, some hidden in the shadows and realms beyond your vision, and others hiding in plain sight. But make no mistake, they will not allow you to destroy the planet they rely on."

Kersius looked around as if to make sure every single person in attendance heard his message loud and clear.

"All of your prophets," he continued, "spoke of love. And if they did not speak of love, then they were either misunderstood... or they were not prophets. So, take my final instruction to heart. It's a simple message. Love one another. Love the planet you live on. Forgive your enemies. That's it." He looked around. "You are all connected—*we* are all connected—in ways you do not comprehend. But with hope, one day you will. You came here lured by a false prophet, perhaps to pursue one whose message years ago was similar to this. And now you have once again received it. For the sake of your species, it is my sincere wish that you take it to heart this time."

Kersius paused for a second, then turned and let the crowd talk amongst themselves. He approached Ariella and Cassandra as Luke stood by.

"Is he dead?" said Ariella. "Is he finally gone?"

"With Valdok, it's always hard to say," said Kersius. "He's an eternal being. At the least, he won't return for many lifetimes. But there are other threats out there. For now, I need to gather survivors. We need to mend."

He redirected his attention to Cassandra.

"You knew me as Gideon. I could not tell you the truth or it could have put you and our daughter in unspeakable danger. But please understand, it had to be you. It could be no one else. I hope one day you can forgive me."

Cassandra smiled and hugged him. "If I knew the stakes, I would've gladly done it all over again."

To Luke's surprise, Kersius redirected his attention to him and smiled.

"Take good care of her, Lucas," said Kersius. "Take care of both of them."

"I will," said Luke, returning the smile. "Though I think they can take care of me." He was surprised Kersius knew his name. Then again, he was surprised by a lot of things these days.

Kersius turned and left just as Wilcox approached with his senior staff—the president and Kilgor in tow. Hargrove and Martinez came to greet them.

"Admiral Hargrove," said Wilcox. "And Captain Martinez."

Hargrove and Martinez saluted him.

"As the only ranking officers I trust quite yet, I'd like you to escort the president and Special Agent Kilgore to our vehicles. Just follow the roped-off section back there to the east. We'll meet you there."

"Roger that, Admiral," said Hargrove.

Wilcox turned to Luke and gave him a pat on the arm. "And thank *you* for your service." He winked and smiled. "We'll catch up later."

After Wilcox turned and left, the president wasted no time pleading with Hargrove.

"Listen Admiral," said the president, "I did what I had to do for the American people. You would've done the same damn thing. Hell, you heard him, I had no idea they were gonna wipe out the whole planet."

"So you made a deal not even knowing they had a bigger card up their sleeve," said Hargrove. "So it was just tit for tat? Americans for tech?"

"I made a deal because that's what I'm good at and it needed to be done. We needed that tech. And it was a damn good deal if they held up their end of the bargain. Nobody would've threatened this country ever again. Listen, nobody did more for this country than me. My base knows it. They won't allow any of this. You want a civil war? Go ahead and—"

"With all due respect, Mr. President," said Hargrove, "shut your damn mouth before I make you disappear and blame it on an alien time bomb."

Luke observed as Hargrove and Martinez whisked the president and Kilgore away. Kilgore was surprisingly silent for once.

Luke turned and smiled, because he now saw a sight for sore eyes. Royster approached. He was helping Brody, who was limping.

"You okay?" said Luke.

"I'll live," said Brody. "I'm a year from retirement, a bum leg's not gonna stop me. Of course, it'll be hard getting back to police work after battling space aliens."

"Well, you did a hell of a job," said Luke. "You both did."

"Kevin here whisked me out of harm's way," said Brody.

"Luke," said Royster, reaching out to shake his hand, "it was an honor to serve with you in Afghanistan, but honestly? That had nothing on this!"

"I think I can agree with you there."

"Do you think they'll ever change?" said Royster. "The people, I mean. Will they do what he said?"

"A few days ago, if you asked me that—how the people would react if the real Messiah came speaking of love and peace? I'd have said most of them would probably crucify him all over again. Now? I'm not so sure. We're entering a new world, my friend."

Royster nodded.

"You give them more credit than I do," said Brody. "But what do I know?"

Luke spotted Ariella approaching, so Royster and Brody

gave him some privacy.

"Luke," said Ariella, looking up at him, "will you be leaving us now?" She was the picture of innocence, hardly the headstrong supreme being she seemed an hour ago.

"Not a chance," he said, bending down. "Listen," he said. "I lost my family. There's nothing I can do about that, but I know they'll always be with me. And it seems God saw fit to give me a new family, too. You and your mom. What do you think?"

Ariella grinned from ear to ear, the way a child should. She was about to say something, but paused.

"I think they want to talk to you," she said.

He looked at her with curiosity as her An'za stone began glowing.

"Put your hands around this," she said, holding up the stone. "Trust me."

Luke did as he asked and everything around him became hazy. He didn't know what was happening to him. Two figures materialized before his eyes. He recognized them at once, though he couldn't believe it.

"Kath," he said. "Kayla. Is it really you?"

He held his arms out and embraced them both. He could feel their warmth. He could sense Kathleen's delicate perfume and Kayla's soft cheek against his.

"It's us, Daddy," said Kayla, sounding as chipper as ever.

"We can only be with you for a little, Luke," said Kathleen. "We want you to know we're proud of you, and there's nothing to fear. Nothing to regret."

"We miss you, Daddy," said Kayla. "But we'll see you again one day."

"I miss you too, sweetheart," said Luke.

"Go be with them," said Kathleen. "They need you."

He nodded. "I wish you could come back," he said.

"No regrets," she said. "Don't be afraid."

A wave of calm washed over him. Before he could say anything, they dematerialized. The world spun as he felt like he was coming out of a trance. He staggered a bit, then gained his footing. His vision began to clear. He felt lighter than air.

"Was that real?" he said to Ariella.

"It was, Luke," she said. "I promise."

"But how—"

"Even I don't know that."

"They said no regrets," he said, still half-dazed. "And then I felt the anger drain from my body. It was as if it was melting away into the air. I felt…"

Cassandra came up from behind him and took his hand.

"Are you okay?" she said.

He nodded and smiled. "Yes, I think I am. We're together now."

He took both of their hands and led them toward the desert clearing as they followed behind the mass exodus—save for the soldiers, who stayed behind to clean up the site. He prayed they took Kersius's message to heart.

"Together," said Cassandra. "I like the sound of that."

They continued walking hand-in-hand until a soldier Luke didn't know came running up to him.

"Sir, I saw you on the news," said the young man, out of breath. He was a Private. "Looks like you were right all along. I just wanted to thank you for helping bring back my family. So… um, well… thanks, Petty Officer, Remington." He reached out his hand.

"Reverend," said Luke, shaking the soldier's hand. "Call me Reverend."

ABOUT THE AUTHORS

Edward Miller is the author of the YA Space Opera novels *Cadets* and *Cadets 2: Ship of the Gods*, as well as the co-author of the time-travel thriller, *The Kronos Interference*, named to the Kirkus Reviews Best of 2012. Edward loves hearing from his readers and can be reached at beameuped@aol.com.

J.B. Manas is the author of the twisty, stylish, award-winning thriller *The Mirror Man*, sci-fi thriller *Atticus*, and co-author of the time-travel thriller *The Kronos Interference*, which Kirkus Reviews called "impressively original" and "[a] tour de force." Manas also writes graphic novels, collaborating with legendary artists and creators from the world of comics.

J.B. loves hearing from his readers and can be reached via email at jb@jbmanas.com. Visit his website at www.jbmanas.com.

OTHER BOOKS BY THE AUTHORS

Books by Edward Miller and J.B. Manas:

The Kronos Interference: *An underwater discovery leads a scientist to travel back in time to kill Hitler, causing a ripple effect he must undo before humanity is erased from the Earth.*
* Named to the Best of 2012 by Kirkus Reviews (starred review)

Books by Edward Miller:

Cadets: *Rival teen cadets on a remote training planet must overcome their differences when they find they're the last resort to save Earth from annihilation by alien invaders looking for their missing comrades.*

Cadets 2: Ship of the Gods: *When a dangerous alien species threatens Earth, the cadets must rely on their former enemy, the Altarrans, to defend the planet while searching for a long-hidden weapon known as the Ship of the Gods.*

Books by J.B. Manas:

The Mirror Man: *In this twisty, stylish thriller, a reclusive writer with the power to read memories is forced by a mysterious stranger to steal government secrets that could send the West back into the dark ages.*
* Winner: Best Sci-Fi Thriller of 2022 (BestThrillers.com)

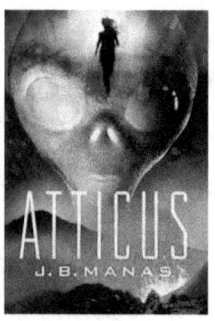

Atticus: *A rookie policewoman must protect a downed pilot who thinks it's 1944 and find out why they're both being hunted by government agents and a Nordic assassin with unearthly powers.*

Visit the authors on Social Media:

Facebook: https://www.facebook.com/MillerandManas/

Facebook: https://www.facebook.com/jbmanas/

Instagram: https://www.instagram.com/jbmanas

Website: https://jbmanas.com/

THE ONE